ELEANOR ARNASON

Winner of the Tiptree award
Mythopoeic award
Spectrum award
HOMer award
and Nebula and Hugo award nominee

"Arnason's wise and engaging stories make you question the things you take for granted. How we love, how we fight, how we live."

—Maureen McHugh, Tiptree and Hugo Award winner

"A great author can write the story of an individual life and make it evoke the large world. But I've rarely seen an evocation so large that it encompasses that world's prehistory as well as its future. Or seen this accomplished in just over twenty thousand words. Arnason is a great author and *Mammoths of the Great Plains* is a great story."

—Karen Joy Fowler, bestselling author of *The Jane Austen Book Club*

"Eleanor Arnason is an amazing writer—direct, committed, and keen-eyed. Her work is always firmly grounded in reality no matter how fantastic that reality may be, and her fondness and respect for her characters infuses her stories with warmth and humor even while she focuses on the grim interplay of power, politics, and the desire of people to lead decent lives. *Mammoths of the Great Plains* is a welcome addition to an admirable body of work."

—Suzy McKee Charnas, Hugo, Nebula and Tiptree Award winner

PM PRESS OUTSPOKEN AUTHORS SERIES

MAMMOTHS
OF THE
GREAT PLAINS

plus...

MAMMOTHS OF THE GREAT PLAINS

plus

Writing Science Fiction
During World War Three

and

"At the Edge of the Future"
Outspoken Interview

ELEANOR ARNASON

PM PRESS | 2010

Eleanor Arnason © 2010
This edition © 2010 PM Press

An earlier version of *Writing Science Fiction During World
War Three* was published in *Ordinary People*, Aqueduct Press,
Seattle, WA, 2005.

ISBN: 978-1-60486-075-7
LCCN: 2009912454

PM Press
P.O. Box 23912
Oakland, CA 94623
PMPress.org

Printed in the USA on recycled paper.

Cover: John Yates/Stealworks.com
Inside design: Josh MacPhee/Justseeds.org

CONTENTS

MAMMOTHS OF THE GREAT PLAINS

Every summer my parents sent me to stay with my grandmother in Fort Yates, North Dakota. I took the rocket train from Minneapolis, waving at Mom and Dad on the platform as the train pulled out, then settling comfortably into my coach seat. I loved my parents, but I also loved to travel, and I was especially fond of the trip to Fort Yates.

We glided north along the Mississippi, gaining speed as we left the city and entered the wide ring of suburbs around Minneapolis and St. Paul. Looking out, I saw scrub woods and weedy meadows, dotted with the ruins of McMansions and shopping malls.

The suburbs had been built on good land, my dad told me, replacing farms, wood lots, lakes and marshes. "A terrible waste of good soil, which could have fed thousands of people; and the land is not easy to reclaim, given all the asphalt and concrete which has been poured over it. That's why we've left it alone. Let time and nature work on it and soften it up!"

Dad's employer, the Agricultural Recovery Administration, might be ignoring the suburbs. But there were people in them. Looking out my window, I saw gardens and tents among the weeds and ruined houses; and there were platforms made of scrap wood along the tracks. The rocket trains didn't stop at the platforms; but local trains did, picking up produce for markets in the city. Now and then I saw an actual person, hanging clothes on a line or riding a bicycle bumpily along a trail.

"Fools," Dad called them and refused to buy their food in the market, though it had passed inspection. I thought the people were romantic: modern pioneers. My grandmother had things to say about pioneers, of course.

North of St. Cloud, the forest began, and I went to the bubble car, riding its lift to the second floor and a new seat with a better view. The forest was second or third growth, a mixture of conifers and hardwoods; and there was a terrible problem with deer. They were a problem on farms as well, though not as much as gen-mod weeds and bugs. Market hunters controlled the deer, in so far as they were controlled. Wolves and panthers would do a better job, my father said; but the farmers didn't like them.

Trees flashed by, light green and dark green, brown if they were dying. The conifers were heat-stressed and vulnerable to parasites and disease. In time the forest would be entirely hardwood. Now and then I saw a gleam of blue: a pond or lake surrounded by forest. Sometimes the train crossed a river.

Around noon we reached the bed of fossil Lake Agassiz, also known as the Red River Valley. The forest ended, and we traveled through farm land, amazingly flat. Trees grew in lines between the fields: windbreaks. They were necessary, given the wind that came off the western plains. The main crops were potatoes and sugar beets. The farmers had to keep changing the varieties they grew as the climate changed, getting hotter. "We're like the Red Queen in *Alice*," Dad said. "Running and running in order to remain in one place."

The train stopped at Fargo-Moorhead, then turned due north, going along the Red River to Grand Forks. Then it turned again. I went to the dining car and ate lunch while we raced west across the North Dakota plain. This was wind farm country. Rows of giant windmills extended as far as I could see. Between them were fields of sunflowers. In the old days, my dad said, the fields had been dotted with pothole lakes and marshes full of wild birds. Most were gone now, the water dried up and the birds flown. In any case, the train moved so rapidly that I couldn't bird watch, except to look at hawks soaring in the dusty blue sky, too far up to identify.

I got off at Minot and stayed the night with my mother's second cousin Thelma Horn. In the morning Thelma put me on a local train that ran south along the Missouri River. There was only one passenger car, hitched to an engine that hauled boxcars and tankers. The track was not nearly as well maintained as the rocket train's line. The local rocked slowly along, stopping often. By late morning we were on the Standing Rock Reservation. There were bison on the hillsides, the only livestock that made sense in short grass prairie, my dad said, and hawks in the sky. If I was lucky, I might see pronghorns or a flock of wild turkeys.

By noon I was at the Fort Yates station. My grandmother waited there, tall and thin and upright, her hair pulled back in a bun and her nose jutting like the nose on the Crazy Horse monument. At home in Minneapolis, I forgot I was part Lakota. Here, looking at my grandmother, I remembered.

She hugged me and took me to her house, an old wood frame as spare and upright as she was. My bedroom was on the second floor, overlooking an empty lot. Grandmother had turned it into a garden, full of native plants that thrived in the dry heat of the western Dakotas. Prairie flowers bloomed among wild grasses. A bird feeder fed native sparrows; and a rail fence hosted meadowlarks, who stood as tall as possible, showing off their bright yellow chests, and sang—oh! so loudly!

What could be better than our breakfasts in the kitchen, the windows open to let in cool morning air? Or the hours when I played with the Fort Yates kids, brown-skinned and black-haired? I was darker than they were; and my hair frizzed, because my dad came from the Ivory Coast. But they were relatives, and we got along most of the time.

In the afternoon, when it was too hot to play, I talked with Grandmother—either in the kitchen as we worked on dinner, or in the parlor under a turning ceiling fan. This is when I learned the story of the mammoths.

o o o

ACCORDING TO GRANDMOTHER, THE trouble began with Lewis and Clark. "We'd heard rumors about what was happening in the east, and the voyageurs had been through our country. Those Frenchmen got everywhere like mice, which is why so many Ojibwa and some Dakota and even Lakota have names like Boisvert, Trudel, Bellecourt and Zephier. But the French were interested in beaver, not our bison and mammoths. We told them if they behaved, they could have safe passage to the Rockies. For the most part, they did behave themselves; and for the most part, we kept our word.

"The thing to remember about the French and the Scots is, they were businessmen. You could reason with them. But the English and Americans were explorers and scientists and farmers searching for new land. People like these are driven by dreams—discovery, investigation, conquest, farms on the short grass prairie where there isn't enough water for trees. No one could reason with them." Grandmother had a Ph.D. in molecular biology from the University of Massachusetts. She was joking, not speaking out of ignorance or disrespect for science.

I'm telling the story the way she told it to me, sitting in her living room in Fort Yates, North Dakota, when I came to visit her on the Standing Rock Reservation in summer. She didn't tell the whole story at once, but piece by piece over days and weeks and from summer to summer. I heard most parts more than once. But I'm going to retell it as a single continuous story; and after this, I'm not going to point out the jokes. There are plenty. Grandmother used to say, "The only way Indians survive is through patience and a strong sense of humor. What a joke the Great Spirit played on us, when it sent Europeans here!"

Anyway, the trouble began that morning in 1805, when Meriwether Lewis became the first white man of English descent to see a mammoth since mammoths died out in England. The animal in question was an adult male, sixty years old or so, older than Meriwether Lewis would ever get to be. It was standing on the bank of the Missouri River drinking water, while its tusks—magnificent ten foot long spirals—shone in the early light. Lewis knew what he was seeing. His neighbor, President Thomas Jefferson, had told him to keep a lookout for mammoths, which white men in the east knew from fossils.

The animal Lewis was looking at was not *Mammuthus columbii*, which had left fossils in the east. Instead this was *Mammuthus missourii*, a smaller descendent. An adult male Columbian mammoth could stand thirteen feet tall and weigh ten tons. The fellow drinking water from the Missouri stood ten feet tall at most and weighed five or six tons.

Did he actually have tusks as long as he was tall? Yes, according to Lewis and later scientists who studied *Mammuthus missourii*. It was, my grandmother said, a classic case of sexual selection.

"In order for a female to achieve reproductive success, she has to be healthy and not too unlucky. This is not true for every species, but it is true of many. In order for a male to breed, he has to impress females and other males. Humans did this with paint, feathers and beads. Look at the paintings by people like George Catlin! Indian men were always gaudier than Indian women. That's because they were trying to proclaim their reproductive fitness. An old-time chief in a war bonnet was exactly like a turkey cock, displaying in the spring."

Don't think Grandmother was speaking disrespectfully of our male ancestors. The wild turkey was her favorite bird; and she felt that little on Earth equaled the sight of a cock spreading his shining bronze tail and making a noise that sounds like "Hubba-hubba."

The tusks of mammoth females stop growing when the animals are twenty-five or thirty, but male tusks keep growing, spiraling out and up until—in some cases—they cross each other.

"All show, of course," my grandmother said. "But what a show!"

Lewis did exactly what you'd expect of a 19th century explorer and scientist. He picked up a gun and shot the mammoth. It was a good shot or possibly lucky. The ball went into the old bull's bright, brown eye. The old fellow screamed in pain and fury, then fell down dead. That was the beginning of the end, my grandmother said.

The expedition butchered the animal, keeping the tusks and skin, which was covered with short, thick, curly fur—most likely light brown; though some mammoths are tan or yellow, and a few are white. They had mammoth steaks for dinner and breakfast, then went on, dragging their boats up river. Most of the meat was left behind to be eaten by wolves and grizzlies. One tusk made it back east to delight President Jefferson. The other was abandoned as too damn heavy. The skin was lost when a boat overturned.

"It was an epic journey," my grandmother said. "And they found many things which Indian people can't remember misplacing, such as the Rocky Mountains. I think you could say that their most famous discovery, even more famous than the Rockies, was living mammoths."

Decades after Lewis and Clark returned to the United States, white people wandered around the west, looking for mastodons, giant ground sloths and sabertooth cats. But all those animals were gone. Only the mammoths had survived into modern times.

There are white scientists who say Indians killed the ice-age megafauna. Grandmother didn't believe this. "If we were so good at killing, why did so many large animals survive? Moose, musk oxen, elk, caribou, bison, mountain lions, five kinds of bear. The turkey, for heaven's sake! They're big; they can't really fly; and though I love them, no one who has seen a turkey try to go through a barbed wire fence can claim they are especially adaptable.

"Why did horses and camels die out in the New World, when other large animals—moose, mammoth, musk ox and bison—survived? Are we to believe that our ancestors preferred eating horse and camel to eating bison? Hardly likely!"

Most likely, the animals that died out were killed by changes in the climate, my grandmother said. Everything got drier and hotter after the glaciers retreated. The mammoth steppe was replaced by short grass prairie. This was no problem for the bison, but mammoths—like elephants—need lots of moisture.

"In the spring when the grass was green and wet, they'd move out onto the plains. Our ancestors would see them in groups of ten or twenty, grazing among the dark-brown bison. By early summer, they retreated to the rivers, especially the Missouri, and fed on shrubs in the bottom lands. Water was always available. Think what it must have been like to float down river in a pirogue or a round bison-hide boat like the ones made by Mandans and Hidatsa! There the mammoths would be, calves and matrons, bathing in the shallows, squirting water on each other.

"Our ancestors always said, be careful of the mammoths when they're by rivers. Wolves, the big ones called bison wolves, and grizzly bears, which used to be a plains animal till white people drove them into the mountains, lurked in the bottom lands. They couldn't harm a healthy adult, but preyed on calves, the old, the injured. Because of this, the mammoths were uneasy close to water."

If I close my eyes now, I can see her living room. The sky is big everywhere in the Dakotas, but west of the Missouri, it gets even bigger; and sunlight comes down through the dry air like a lance. In Grandmother's house, it came through white gauze curtains that fluttered in the wind and danced in spots on her linoleum floor. The furniture in the room was straight and spare, like Grandmother and her house: a kitchen table, four kitchen chairs and a rocker, all old and scratched, but solid wood that Grandmother kept polished. On the floor, along with dancing spots of sunlight, was a genuine oriental rug, the edges frayed and the pile worn flat. Grandmother bought it in an antique store in Minneapolis. She liked the faded colors and the pattern, geometric, like our Lakota patterns.

"The Chinese and Asian Indians make carpets like gardens; but people from dry, wide-open countries— the people in Central Asia and here—like geometry."

Her most treasured belonging was a mammoth tusk about three feet long. The ivory was honey-colored and carved with horsemen chasing bison. She held it on her lap while she told me stories, stroking the tusk's gentle curve and the incised lines.

"There were two young men, hunters in the days before horses and guns; and they were out on the prairie, looking for something to kill. All they had were spears with stone tips and a dog dragging a travois. If you think it was easy hunting this way in a world full of bison, mammoths, wolves and grizzlies, then you haven't given serious consideration to the question.

"The young men thought they might be able to sneak up on a bison disguised as wolves, which the bison don't usually fear, or find a mammoth weakened by drought. It was midsummer and so dry that many streams and small rivers were empty.

"But they had no luck. Exhausted and discouraged, they made camp, tying the dog securely, since it might become food soon, if they didn't find anything else. They ate the last of their pemmican and drank water dug from a river bed, then slept.

"When they woke, the moon was up and full. Two maidens in white dresses stood at the edge of their camp. Never had they seen girls so lovely. One man was clever enough to recognize spirits when he saw them; he greeted the women respectfully. But the other man was stupid and rude. Getting up, he tried to grab one of the women. She turned and walked quickly across the moonlit prairie. He followed. When they were almost out of sight, the woman turned into a white mammoth, her fur shining like snow in the moonlight. But this didn't make the rude man pause. He followed the mammoth till both of them were gone.

"The second woman said, 'That is my sister, White Mammoth Calf Woman. Your companion will follow her till he's out of this world entirely. But you have greeted me with respect, so I'll teach you the way to hunt bison and how to use every part of the animal, so your people won't be hungry in the future. Remember, though, not to hunt the mammoths, since your companion has made them angry. If you hunt them in spite of my warning, you'll make the bison angry as well; and they and the mammoths will leave.'

"Then she taught him everything about bison. He thanked her gratefully; and she turned to go. 'What is your name?' the polite man asked. In answer, she turned into a snow-white bison calf and ran off across the plain.

"After that," my grandmother said, "our ancestors hunted bison, but not mammoths. There were practical reasons for this decision. Can you imagine trying to attack a full-sized mammoth on foot with no weapon except a spear? The calves were less formidable, but their mothers and aunts protected them; and the males formed groups of their own.

"The only truly vulnerable mammoths were juvenile males, after they'd been driven from the maternal herd, while they were wandering around alone, confused and ignorant. People did hunt them sometimes, but that didn't lead to extinction.

"Maybe, using fire and stampeding, we could have killed mammoth herds. But we didn't, because White Bison Calf Woman had warned us."

Then Grandmother told another story. "There was a man who went hunting in a hard time, a drought. He came on a huge bull mammoth with magnificent tusks. The animal had a foot that was broken or dislocated.

"'Brother mammoth,' the man said. 'My family is starving. Will you give your flesh to me?'

"The mammoth considered, waving his trunk around and smelling the dusty air. 'All right,' he said finally. 'But I want to keep my tusks. Call me vain or sentimental, if you like. They mean a lot to me; and I want them to stay where I've lived. Take everything else—my flesh, my skin, even my bones—but leave my tusks here.'

"The man agreed. The mammoth let him strike a killing blow.

"When the mammoth was dead, the man brought his wife to butcher the carcass. 'We can't leave the tusks here,' the woman said. 'Look at how huge they are, how perfectly curved.'

"'I promised,' said the man. But the woman wouldn't listen. She chopped the tusks out of the mammoth's skull. They took everything home: the flesh, the skin covered with tawny curling hair, the tusks.

"After that, the woman had trouble sleeping. The mammoth came to her, wearing his flesh and skin, but with two bloody wounds where his tusks should have been. 'What have you done?' he asked. 'Why have you stolen the only things I asked to keep?'

"Gradually, lack of sleep wore the woman down. Finally, she died. Soon after that, her husband visited another village and saw a maiden of remarkable beauty. 'What will you take for her?' he asked the girl's father, who was an old man, still handsome and imposing, except for his missing teeth.

"'Your famous mammoth tusks,' the old man said.

"The warrior was reluctant, but he had never seen a woman like this one; and she seemed more than willing to go with him. Grudgingly, he agreed to the bargain, went home and returned with the mammoth tusks. The old man took the splendid objects and caressed them. 'I will use them to frame my door,' he said. This was a Mandan or Hidatsa village, as I forgot to mention. Our neighbors along the Missouri often took tusks from drowned mammoths and used them as frames for the doors of their log and dirt houses. We didn't, of course, since we lived in tipis in those days.

"The warrior and his new wife took off across the plain. At their first camp, the warrior said, 'I want to have sex with you.' He'd been thinking about nothing else for days.

"'You people!' said the maiden. 'You never learn!' Rising, she turned into a white mammoth. Her fur shone like snow in the moonlight, as did her small female tusks. 'You asked for help from my kinsman, then took the only things he wanted to keep, though he was willing to give you everything else, even his life. Now he has his tusks back. You will get nothing more from me.' She turned and moved rapidly over the prairie."

"If we aren't supposed to kill mammoths and take their tusks, how do you have that one on your lap?" I asked when I was ten and full of questions, which I had learned to ask in a experimental school in Minneapolis.

"The point of the story," said Grandmother, "is to ask permission, listen to the answer with respect and keep the promises you make. The tusk on my lap is from a juvenile. One of our ancestors may have killed it before it joined a male group; if it was female, then it died of injury or drought, and our ancestor scavenged the tusks.

"If it was a young cow, then our ancestor may have made a mistake by carving a hunting scene on the tusk. But I don't know any stories about the ancestor; most likely he didn't come to harm, as he would have, if he'd done something seriously wrong." It was hard to tell with Grandmother, because of her irony, if she meant a statement like this. On the one hand, she was a scientist and a woman who believed that much harm happened in the world and went unpunished. On the other hand, she took the old stories seriously. "There is more than one way to organize knowledge; and more than one way to formulate truth; and with time and patience, persistence and luck, justice can prevail."

There was a story about the fate of Meriwether Lewis, which Grandmother told me. He came back from his journey a famous man, who became governor of the Missouri Territory; but despair overtook him. He died of suicide at the age of thirty-five, alone while traveling along the Natchez Trace. On a scrap of paper in his pocket were his last words. 'Mammoths,' he wrote in an agitated scrawl. 'Indians.' That was all, though—being Lewis—he misspelled both 'mammoth' and 'Indian.'"

"What does the message mean?" I asked.

"Who can say?" my grandmother replied. "Maybe it was a warning of some kind. 'Treat mammoths as I have done, and you will end like me.' Or maybe he was drunk. He had a problem with alcohol and opium. In any case, no one paid attention. More white people came up the Missouri—scientists, explorers, traders, hunters, English noblemen, Russian princes. They all shot mammoths; or so it seemed to our ancestors, who watched with horror. We tried to warn the Europeans, but they didn't listen. Maybe they didn't care. At some point, we realized they had an idea of the way our country ought to be: full of white farmers on farms like the ones in Europe, though our land is nothing like England or France. The mammoths would be gone and the bison and us. If you look at the paintings done along the Missouri in the 19th century, it always seems to be sunset. The small mammoth herds, the vast bison herds, the Indians are always heading west into the sunset, vanishing from the plains.

"Some of the tusks went to hang on walls in England and Moscow. Others went to museums in the east, along with entire skeletons and skins. The American Museum of Natural History in New York has a stuffed herd in their Hall of Mammoths. I've seen it. You ought to go some day.

"As the century went on, the Europeans began to take animals alive. In almost every case, these were calves whose mothers had been shot. Mammoth Bill Cody had two in his Wild West Show. Sitting Bull used to visit with them, during the year the great Lakota spent with the show. People say he talked with them, while they curled their trunks around his arms and searched in his clothing for hidden food. We don't know what they told him. He came away looking sad and grim.

"By the end of the 19th century, the only mammoths left were in circuses and zoos, except for a small herd in the Glacier Park area. At most, four hundred animals were left. The ones in circuses were calves. The ones in zoos were a mixture of old and young, though all had grown up in captivity. Their culture—which they used to learn from elders, as did we—was gone, except in the Glacier Park herd, which still preserved some of its ancestral wisdom. In this, the Glacier mammoths were like our neighbors the Blackfeet. Louis W. Hill, the son of the Empire Builder, encouraged the Blackfeet to maintain their old ways, in order to present tourists coming out on the Great Northern Railroad with an authentic western experience. Historians have said many bad things about the Hill family, but they protected the mammoths and the Blackfeet from the rest of white civilization.

"White Bison Calf Woman's warning were proved true. As the mammoths disappeared, so did the far more numerous bison. By century end, only a few hundred of them remained, though they had roamed the west in herds of millions; and we all know what happened to Indians. Because I don't like being angry, I am not going to recount that story. In any case, I'm talking about mammoths.

"At this point, the story turns to my own grandmother, who was your great-great-grandmother. Her first name was Rosa, and her real last name was Red Mammoth, but she was adopted by missionaries when she was very young and took their name, which was Stevens. They sent her east to school, and she studied veterinary medicine, becoming the first woman to receive a DVM from her college. Although Rosa had little experience with Indian culture, she had good dreams. In one of these a mammoth came to her, a white female.

"'I want you to devote your life to mammoth care,' the animal said. 'We have reached the point where anything could kill us: a disease gotten from domestic animals, ailments caused by inbreeding or a change of heart among white men. What if Louis W. Hill decides there is a better way to promote his railroad? In addition, most of us no longer know how to behave.'

"'I certainly want to work with large animals,' Rosa said. 'But I was thinking of cattle and horses, not mammoths. I know nothing about them.'

"'You can learn,' the mammoth said. 'What you don't find out from the herd in Glacier can be discovered by studying elephants, who are our closest relatives. If we are not saved, the bison will die as well; and I don't hold out a lot of hope for Indians. These white people are crazy. There's no way to farm the high plains or to raise European cattle on them. This country is too dry and cold. Yes, the white people can come here and ruin everything—overgraze the prairie, drain the rivers or fill them with poison, mine and log the sacred Black Hills. Once they have finished, they will have to leave or live like scavengers in the wreckage they have made. The only way to make a living here is through bison and us.' As you might be able to tell, granddaughter, the mammoth was angry. Like their relatives the elephants, mammoths can feel grief and hold serious grudges.

"Rosa was no fool. It was pretty obvious this was no ordinary dream. The white mammoth was some kind of spirit. She agreed to the animal's request. Because she was Lakota and had a college degree, she was able to get a job at Glacier Park. This was in 1911, when the park had just opened and the famous tourist lodges were not yet built.

"She spent three years at Glacier. The job proved frustrating. The herd wasn't growing. The animals ranged too far, maybe in response to tourists, who wanted nothing more than to photograph these spectacular and shy animals. Once out of the park, ranchers shot them, claiming that the mammoths stampeded cattle. In the park, they were occasionally shot by poachers and even by park rangers, if they went into musth, which is a reproductive frenzy, more common among males than females.

"The animals were less fertile than elephants. Rosa couldn't tell if this was a natural difference between the two species; or if it was due to inbreeding or stress. The fact that mammoths seized cameras whenever they were able, flung them to the ground and stamped on them, suggested that part of the problem was stress. She was unable to convince the park administration to outlaw cameras.

"Finally, discouraged and thinking of leaving her job, she had another dream. A woman wearing a white deerskin dress came to her. The woman was middle aged and obviously Indian, her skin dark, her hair straight and black. Her dress had white beadwork over the shoulders. She had on white moccasins, decorated like her dress with white beadwork. Long earrings made of ivory hung from her ears. 'This isn't working,' she told Rosa.

"'I know,' Rosa replied.

"'We need a new plan,' the woman continued. 'Do you know about the mammoths which have been found frozen in ice in eastern Russia?'

"'Yes.'

"'Learn everything you can about them. They died thousands of years ago, but have been preserved well enough so flesh and skin and hair remains. Maybe it will be possible to revive them someday. White men are ingenious, especially when it comes to doing things that are unnatural.' The woman paused. Rosa blinked, and the woman became a mammoth with snow-white fur and ice-blue eyes. The mammoth waved her trunk back and forth in the air like a conductor directing an orchestra. Her pale eyes seemed to look into the far distance. The dream ended."

My grandmother got up and went to the bathroom, then took iced tea out of her refrigerator. It had lemon juice already in it, along with sugar and mint from her garden. She poured us both glasses and sat down again in her rocker. The tusk was back hanging on her wall, along with other mementos which she had tacked up: pictures of relatives, including my mom and dad, a bunch of postcards of places in the Black Hills. Not Mount Rushmore, but Spearfish Canyon and the Needles Road and Crazy Horse monument. Lastly, there was a necklace of silver beads hanging from a nail. A tiny, beautifully carved mammoth hung from the necklace, made of pipestone with turquoise eyes.

We sipped the tea. Grandmother rocked.

"What happened next?" I asked.

"To Rosa? She went to Russia, taking the eastern route via China since World War I had begun. Louis W. Hill funded her trip. He was worried about the Glacier Park mammoths, too. In his own strange way—the way of an entrepreneur, who must possess what he loves and make money from it, if possible—he loved his Blackfeet and their mammoths.

"Rosa ended in Siberia in a town with a name I can't remember now, though it's on the tip of my tongue. Maybe it'll come to me. Old age, Emma! It comes to all of us, and even gene tech can't repair all the damage! The houses were built of logs, and the streets were dirt. It was like being in the wild west, she told me, except this was the wild east. The people were drunk Russians and brown-skinned natives, who looked like Indians or

Inuit. It was easy to see where we Indians had come from, Rosa told me. The native people drank also. It's a curse that goes around the North Pole and among many native peoples.

"Pine forest rose around the town. The trees were huge and dark and shut out the sky. Rosa said that's what she missed most in Siberia, the sky. Our kinfolk, the Dakota, were driven out of pine forest by the Ojibwa, who were armed with European guns. The Dakota are still angry about this. Rosa said, in her opinion the pine forest was no loss; though the sugar maples and wild rice lakes might be something to mourn.

"She was in Siberia through most of the war, studying with a Russian scientist who was an expert on frozen mammoths. He was a young man, but he'd lost toes to frostbite and walked with a limp and a cane, so the Russian army wasn't interested in him. A small fellow, Rosa told me, no taller than she was, wiry, with yellow hair and green eyes slanted above cheekbones that looked Indian. Sergei Ivanoff.

"This is the hardest part of Rosa's story to tell," my grandmother said. "I've never been to Siberia, and Rosa kept her own counsel about much that happened there. I imagine them in a log cabin, lamps glowing in the midwinter darkness, studying the mammoth tissues that they'd found. Sergei had brought equipment with him from the west, so they could stain the tissue and examine it under microscopes.

"As far as she and Sergei could determine, given the primitive science of the time, all the tissue they examined had been damaged—most likely by the process of freezing, then thawing, then freezing again. Ice is a remarkable solid, less dense than its liquid form. As the water in the mammoth cells froze, it expanded. The cell walls ruptured; the delicate natural machinery within was broken past any repair they could imagine.

"For the most part, they were able to ignore the war. Travel was interrupted, but neither of them were planning to travel. Sergei wanted more scientific supplies, but he was too poor to order them. Rosa sent letters to Louis W. Hill, asking for money. They weren't answered. She didn't know if Hill had received them.

"In 1917 the war led to the famous Russian Revolution. This happened in the far west, in places like St. Petersburg. Only rumors reached them in their cabin. The local trappers and hunters said, Tsar Nicholas had died and been replaced with a new tsar named Lenin-and-Trotsky.

"One evening soldiers arrived on horses. They heard them coming, shouting to each other.

"Sergei said, 'Take our notes and hide. I'll deal with this.'

"Her arms full of paper, Rosa darted behind their cabin. It was winter, snow falling thickly. A mammoth carcass, thousands of years old, lay in a shack. Rosa climbed in among the ancient bones and skin. She crouched down, shivering. Did voices speak, muffled by the snow? She wasn't certain. At last the silence was broken by two loud, sharp noises like doors slamming.

"'Aaay,' Rosa whispered. In her mind she prayed to her foster family's deity, the God of Episcopalians. The door to the shack opened. A man spoke in a language she didn't understand: Russian.

"She and Sergei had always conversed in German, the language of science, or French, the language of civilization.

"Instead of entering, the man went elsewhere, leaving the shack door open. An icy wind blew in.

Rosa cowered in the middle of the mammoth. A vision came to her: she was in a hut. The walls were made of mammoth jaws. The roof beams were tusks. A dung fire burned on the dirt floor. Across the fire from her was an ancient woman, her long hair gray, her dress smoke-darkened and greasy.

"'Stay here a while,' the woman said. 'Till the soldiers are gone.'

"'Who are they?' Rosa asked.

"'Red Guards or White Guards, what does it matter? They are ignorant and desperate. Tsar Nicholas is dead, and his son will never rule. Tsar Lenin-and-Trotsky will not achieve the wonderful things he—they dream of. Things must get worse before they get better.'

"Rosa didn't like to hear this, but she remained in the mammoth hut, which seemed warmer than her shack. The old woman fed dried dung into the fire. Her eyes were milky blue. Blind, maybe. Rosa couldn't tell.

"Finally the old woman said, 'You'll freeze to death if you stay here. The soldiers have gone. Get up and go back to the cabin.'

"Obedient, Rosa stood and walked to the hut door. A mammoth skin hung over it. As Rosa raised her hand to push the skin aside, the woman said, 'Remember one thing.'

"'Yes?'

"'The cold has done a marvelous job of preserving the bodies of my kin. But—like the revolution that is now beginning to fail—the job has not been good enough. What can make it better, Rosa? Don't give up! Persist! And think!'

"Rosa turned to ask for more information, but the old woman was gone. For a moment, she stared at the empty hut. Then the dung fire vanished; and she found herself standing, numb with cold, at the entrance to the mammoth shack. Snow fell around her, kissing her cheeks. She couldn't feel her hands. Her feet were barely able to move. Stumbling, she crossed the space to the cabin's back door.

"Inside was chaos: spilled books, overturned furniture. Sergei lay on the floor in a pool of blood. The cabin stove was still lit, thank God. Red fire shone through the cracks around its door, and the cabin felt warm. She knelt by Sergei. Blood covered half his face, coming from a wound in his forehead. There was more blood on his carefully laundered, white shirt. His pince-nez glasses lay on the floor beside him, one lens shattered.

"'Aaay, Sergei,' she moaned.

"A green eye opened. 'Rosa,' he whispered. 'They didn't find you.'

"'No,' she replied, her heart full of joy.

"Examining him, she discovered he'd been shot twice. One bullet had gone through his shoulder. The other had grazed his head. Eager for loot, the soldiers had not given him a close look after he fell. Instead, they'd gathered the jar that held their little store of money; Sergei's lovely instruments, made of brass and steel; her jewelry and most of their warm clothes. Half their books had gone into the stove to warm the soldiers while they searched the cabin.

"Once he was bandaged, Sergei said, 'This is the end. We're going to China. Do you have our notes?'

"Rosa hurried back to the mammoth shack and found them, fallen among huge bones and shreds of hairy skin. Oddly enough, they smelled of smoke, though there hadn't been a fire in the shack. She carried the papers back to the cabin. She and Sergei packed what remained of their belongings, put on their skis and set out for the nearest town.

"Their journey to Beijing was long and arduous. In spite of many difficulties they made it safely. In Beijing they parted, Rosa going home to America, while Sergei remained to study Chinese fossils. It was he, along with Teilhard de Chardin, who discovered the remains of Peking Man and he who carried those remarkable relics to safety when the Japanese invaded China.

"Rosa never saw him again, though she carried a memento back with her. Do you know what it was, Emma?"

"No."

"Think!"

I frowned and tried of think of something Russian. "A samovar?"

Grandmother laughed. "It was a baby. By the time Rosa returned to America, she knew she was pregnant, though it didn't show when she reported to Hill. A good thing, since he was a fierce moralist.

"Do you know who the baby was, Emma?"

I could tell the question was serious and thought hard. "Your mother?"

"Yes. The father was Sergei. You get your green eyes from him and the way they slant over your cheekbones. If you are lucky, you will inherit some of his intelligence and commitment to work."

"Oh." Grandmother had only two grandfathers, which made her unusual. Most people I knew had three or four. One had come from the Rosebud Reservation. I'd seen several pictures of him: a tall young man, his black hair cut short, looking stiff and awkward in his white clothing. In some of the pictures, he was next to his parents, who dressed in the old Indian way, blankets around their bent shoulders. In other pictures he was with his pretty young wife, who was mixed race and had light-colored eyes, striking even in an old photograph. They had only one child who lived, Grandmother told me.

I had seen a single picture of my grandmother's other grandfather: an old man with white hair and a trim, white beard.

"He's old in the photo," I said.

"Sergei? Yes. It was taken years later, when he won the Nobel Prize for Medicine. Rosa clipped it out of a magazine."

"He never even wrote?" I asked.

Grandmother paused a long while. "I never knew for certain," she said at last. "Rosa kept her own counsel.

"Once she was back in Montana, Rosa reported to Louis W. Hill. By this time, he was seriously worried. A disease had killed all the mammoths in the Ringling Brothers Circus. Neither the circus veterinary staff nor the scientists brought in had been able to identify the disease, though it was suspected that it came from the circus elephants; several Indian elephants became ill at the same time, and one died. Now we know it was a herpes virus, which infects African elephants. It's harmless to them, but can cause a serious illness in Indian elephants. We have a vaccine now; before that was developed, the disease was 100 percent fatal to mammoths.

"Thus far, Hill told my grandmother, this was an isolated incident. None the less, he had taken precautions. Circus trains were not allowed to use the section of Northern Pacific's high line which went through Glacier. The park lodges had been instructed to hire no one who admitted to a circus past; and law officers in nearby towns were asked to report any carnivals to the park administration. This was not enough to keep Hill happy. He dug into his pocket and personally paid for an elite group of specially trained mammoth wranglers, who watched the animals and made sure that tourists saw them from a distance. Of course, there were stories about the wranglers in newspapers and magazines; Hill had a genius for marketing. There was even a movie that starred Tom Mix as an outlaw trying to make an honest life as a wrangler. *Sagebrush and Mammoths.* I think that's the right name.

"Still, Hill remained concerned. What if some miserable little carnival managed to elude his precautions and get close to the park? An infected elephant might get lose and wander into the park, or a roaming mammoth might find the circus. What if an infected tourist managed to get close to a mammoth? He could hardly prevent tourists from coming to Glacier; and there was no way to check their backgrounds. The disease might be like rabies, which can infect many kinds of mammals. It might leap from elephants to elk or prairie dogs. Who could say?

"My grandmother thought Hill was worrying too much. More serious, it seemed to her, was the herd's reproductive rate and the danger of inbreeding. Like elephants, mammoths had long gestation periods. They produced single children, and the children had long childhoods. This meant that the Glacier herd was increasing very slowly; and fear of infection meant that they could not introduce genetic variety by bringing in new animals. But she said nothing about this. Instead, she listened—silent and impassive—while Hill paced up and down his private railway car, explaining his concerns. Electric lanterns shone on polished mahogany, dark velvet, oriental carpets and gilded picture frames. The art within the frames was minor. Unlike J. P. Morgan, Hill was not a connoisseur.

"He was stern-looking man, with a trim, white beard. My grandmother said the picture of Sergei when he received the Nobel Prize reminded her of Hill a little. He wore a buttoned vest, even in Glacier; though here in the west he wore jodhpurs and high boots, instead of suit pants and shoes. A battered western hat lay on a chair, along with a drover's coat. His glasses were gold-rimmed pince-nez.

"He stopped finally and asked her to report on her trip. She did, though much was left out.

"'What conclusions have you come to?' he asked. 'Have you learned anything useful, or have I wasted my money?'

"Rose had spent her journey home thinking. 'I believe the secret of saving the mammoths is refrigeration.'

"Hill frowned. 'Explain yourself, Miss Stevens!'

Rosa took a deep breath and continued. "'With luck, you may be able to maintain the herd in Glacier. But it is small; the total population of mammoths alive on Earth is small; and we now know that a disease fatal to the mammoths exists. We need a second plan, a position to which we can fall back, if the worst happens.'

"'Yes?'

"'I would like you to consider two things, sir. First is the remarkable history of the previous century. Consider how much was discovered, how many advances in human knowledge were made! Pasteur and Edison are only two of the geniuses who have transformed the world as we know it. Surely this present century will provide us with comparable discoveries and advances.'

"Hill nodded abruptly. 'Go on.'

"'Second, consider how well preserved the Siberian mammoths are—and for how long—in spite of imperfect conditions. It is my belief that freezing and thawing have damaged the Siberian tissue beyond hope of repair. But it ought to be possible to find a more efficient method of freezing flesh than that provided by a glacier! If we could find a way to freeze tissue samples without damaging the delicate machinery of the cells; and if we could then maintain the tissue samples at a constant temperature, without the freezing and thawing which has done so much harm to the Siberian tissue, then someday—not now, but later in this wonderful new century—it may become possible to start the cellular machinery in motion and reanimate the frozen flesh.'

"'Balderdash' said Hill. He paced the length of the railway car, picked up a riding crop and paced back to her, hitting the crop against his boot. Thwack! Thwack! Thwack! 'I hired you to give me solid science, not ideas out of scientific romances! This plan belongs in the mind of Mr. H. G. Wells, not in the mind of a scientist or in the mind of practical businessman.'

"'Well, then,' said Rosa. 'Consider how useful a really good refrigerated rail car would be for your business. If you could bring the fruits of the west—unspoiled! in perfection condition!—to Chicago and the eastern markets—'

"Hill paused and laid the riding crop down on a mahogany table. Then he paced up and down the car several more times. Finally he stopped in front of a bell jar which contained a pair of beaded moccasins. He tapped the jar top gently. 'In spite of all my efforts, in my heart of hearts I believe my Blackfeet are doomed. Progress can't be stopped. Those in its way will be tossed aside, like a bison standing on a rail line when the express comes through. The future belongs to Anglo-American civilization. The Blackfeet, the bison, my mammoths all belong to an age which is ending or has already ended. But you are right about the usefulness of a really good refrigerated rail car; and modern science ought to be able to find something better than a car full of hay and blocks of ice. I will take your advice and invest in refrigeration; and you—Miss Stevens—can continue your work on mammoth tissue. I will do what I can for the mammoths.'

"Rosa found herself grinning. 'Yes, sir!'

"Why did he love the mammoths so strongly?" my grandmother asked. "I have never been able to decide. Was it their rugged power and persistence? Or the sense that they were survivors from a past age, as he was, the 20th century son of a fierce 19th century father? Whatever his reason, Hill established a research foundation devoted to the study of refrigeration. You must have seen it. It's in St. Paul. A fine example of Art Deco architecture. The tile facade with trumpeting mammoths is especially distinguished.

"While the building was being planned, Rosa went to visit her relatives on the Standing Rock Reservation. My mother was born there. When Rosa returned to work, she left Clara with her Lakota relatives. This was hard to do, but she knew that Hill would not approve of an illegitimate child or a scientist who was also a mother. She refused to give up her research. The mammoths had spoken to her. She would not ignore their advice.

"She wasn't a religious person. The faith she learned as a child faded over time; and she never found another one. But she took her dreams seriously, though she wasn't sure where they came from. Maybe from her unconscious, as Freud and his followers argued; or maybe from a collective unconscious, as other psychologists had argued. In any case, Rosa knew, dreams could provide insight into scientific problems. The structure of benzene came to its discoverer—drat it! I have forgotten the man's name!—in a dream."

Grandmother got up and went to the bathroom again, then refilled our glasses with iced tea. The light coming through the lace curtains came at a lower angle now and had the rich gold of late afternoon. I was getting tired. But I had been raised to listen when elders talked. There were things to be learned here in Fort Yates which I could never learn in my experimental school.

Grandmother settled back in her rocker. "Rosa settled in St. Paul and began work at the Hill Institute. She was Indian and looked it; and she was female. Obviously there were problems at the Institute and in the city. Dislike of Indians goes deep in this part of the country; and at that time there were plenty of people in Minnesota who remembered the Great Sioux Uprising of 1862. Twenty-nine of our Dakota kinsmen were hanged for their part in the uprising, though not all of those who were hanged had taken part. Be that as it may, it was the largest mass execution in the history of the United States.

"Rosa encountered prejudice and difficulty; but the good opinion of Louis W. Hill went a long way in St. Paul in the 1920s. With him standing behind her, she met and overcame every adversity.

"She never married, possibly because she was Indian. White men were reluctant to marry an Indian woman; and there were not many Indian men with her education. Her child remained on Standing Rock. She visited Clara—your great-grandmother—as often as possible, but they were never close. The girl regarded one of Rosa's cousins as her true mother, her mother of the heart. This saddened Rosa, as she told me in her extreme old age. Do you want more iced tea?"

I said no.

"In 1929, the stock market collapsed—as you ought to know, Emma. You've studied some history."

"I do know."

"What did you learn?"

"Never buy on margin."

"That's true enough," said Grandmother and nodded her head. "But there's more to be learned from 1929, as you find out when you're older. At the time the market fell, Louis W. Hill was heavily invested. He was trying to buy control of several west coast rail lines, so he could extend his father's empire into California. By now he had the best refrigerated rail cars in the world; and he wanted to fill them with California produce.

"He was lucky. He didn't go broke when the market crashed. But he had a hard time until the Second World War began. His attention turned from Glacier and the Hill Institute to saving the Great Northern Railroad. The Institute's funds were sharply reduced. Research came to a halt. Rosa ended as a maintenance person, who made sure doors were locked and lights off and the freezers containing the mammoth tissue on. There was still enough money to pay the power bill. Louis W. Hill did not forget the Institute entirely.

"I asked Rosa once if she had felt despair in that period. She said, 'I had a job, which was more than millions had, and I was able to keep an eye on my tissue samples.' She was a stoic woman, who kept much to herself, maybe because she lived between two worlds. Who could she confide in, being Indian by descent and white by culture?"

I sort of understood this, since my dad was mixed

race. But things had been worse back in the 20th century. I knew that.

"In 1938, in the depths of Great Depression, the herd in Glacier became infected with the same disease which had killed the Ringling and Lincoln Park mammoths. To this day, no one knows how the virus got to Glacier. Millions of people were on the move, looking for work. Many rode the rails; and some camped in Glacier. The rangers drove them out. But the park was large and the times troubled. It was not possible to keep all the hobos out. Obviously, none of these people were traveling with an elephant; and as far as Rosa was able to find out, none of them came into contact with the Glacier mammoths.

"Many years later I became interested in the question at a time when I was between research projects. I did a search on hobos and mammoths, using one of the CDC epidemiology programs. Rosa had no such resource, of course. The program did not find an epidemiological connection between hobos and mammoths, but I did find this." Grandmother got up stiffly and went to her computer. It was on a wood side table, its monitor like a glass flower on a curving blue stalk. The keyboard lay to one side, where Grandmother had pushed it while working directly on the screen. As she approached the screen lit up. She touched it lightly with a bony finger.

"You ought to be interested, Emma, since your father plays the blues. This is a WPA recording made in Kansas City in 1936. It's the only recording Frypan Charlie Harrison ever made, and the only time this song was ever recorded." She touched the computer two more times. A guitar began to play old-fashioned country blues, the real thing, but on a really bad instrument.

I could tell from the sound. My dad wouldn't have touched a guitar that sounded like that. Grandmother sat down.

A man's voice—thin and cracked and distant—began to sing:

> Hard times is here, hardest I ever did see.
> Hard times is here, hardest I ever did see.
> Feels like a big bull mammoth stepped on me.
>
> Been riding the rails, looking to earn some pay.
> I been riding the rails, looking to earn some pay.
> That big bull mammoth keeps getting in my way.
>
> Blackbird flying and shining in the sun.
> Blackbird flying and shining in the sun.
> Won't get no rest till my last day is done.

There was more guitar playing, then the recording ended. The computer monitor went dark.

"The recording could have been made to sound like a modern recording," Grandmother said. "For that matter, the technology we have now could make Frypan Charlie sound like a far better blues singer than he was, someone out of the past like Robert Johnson or a present day singer like Delhi John Patel. But this is from the Smithsonian Collection. It sounds the way it would have, if you'd played the original recording right after it was made in 1936. The notes say 'big bull mammoth' is probably a reference to the private police employed by railroads in the 19th and 20th centuries. Though it may also refer to the economic system that was treating Charlie so badly. In any case, the song isn't about Rosa's animals. But I like it. It's the single thing we know about Charlie. He shows up in no other recording."

She was silent for a while, her bony hands folded in her lap and her bright blue eyes gazing right through the living room wall, it seemed to me, into the west river distance. There was no one in my life like her then, and I have never found a replacement for her.

"I especially like the stanza about the blackbird. It reminds me of redwinged blackbirds in the spring. They show up before the marshes turn green, and each male grabs hold of the tallest dry stalk he can find and hangs there, as visible as he can make himself. 'I'm here,' he sings. 'This is me. This is my individual song.'

"That was Charlie's individual song. He's lucky— and we're lucky—that someone recorded it.

"For the next three years, Rosa struggled to save the mammoths. It was to no avail. In 1941, the last Glacier mammoth—a young, pregnant female named Minerva—passed on, with Rosa in attendance. A few animals still remained in zoos around the world, but not enough to form a breeding population. The species was doomed.

"She had wired Hill when the mammoth began to fail. He arrived a day after Minerva's death. Rosa had already removed the fetus and put it into a refrigerator car to be shipped back to St. Paul. She was doing an autopsy of the mother when Hill walked in, dressed in an eastern suit with an eastern hat in his hand.

"He stood for a moment, staring at the corpse, small for a mammoth, but still large.

"'That's it,' he said finally. 'It's over.'

"'We have the tissue samples,' said Rosa. 'And I have frozen every infant that died.'

"He laughed harshly. 'I never believed in your idea of saving the mammoths through refrigeration; but the advice you gave me—to establish the

Institute—was excellent, as is the work you have done on freeze-drying.'

"I forgot to mention that," my grandmother said. "As I told you. Rosa's research in Siberia suggested that water was the culprit in the destruction of mammoth cells. Therefore she had investigated ways to freeze tissue in extremely dry conditions, so as to reduce the amount of water in the cells. She was not able to solve the problem of cellular destruction; but other scientists at the Institute became interested in her work as a method of preserving food.

"Hill had failed in his attempt to move south into California. First the crash slowed him, then that damned communist Franklin Roosevelt was elected, bringing trust busters like a hoard of Visigoths to Washington. Hill could see the writing on the wall; and looking across the Mississippi to the grain mills in Minneapolis, he could see there was a lot of money to be made in food. He gave up on the idea of a western railroad monopoly. Instead, Great Northern diversified into food processing. No matter how bad the times got, people still had to eat.

"His first product was the Pemmican line of dried food, designed to be inexpensive and durable. It came off the production line for the first time in 1940; and the U.S. Army became his first important customer. Along with Spam, another Minnesota product, Pemmican brand dried meat, fruit and vegetables helped to win the war. According to G.I. lore, Pemmican had a thousand uses. You could eat it, use it for shingles or to resole boots, for dry flooring in a tent, as shrapnel in a cannon or flak when dropped from a plane.

"After the war, Great Northern Food Products introduced the Glacier line of frozen vegetables. The packages featured romantic paintings of the national park: Hill's beloved Blackfeet, elk, bison, bears, and the vanished mammoths.

"By this time the Hill Institute was back in business, and Rosa was a senior scientist. She might not have been able to save the mammoths, but her work had been key to development of frozen foods. Louis Hill was grateful, though he held the patents to the freezing process, and she never got any royalties. I don't think she minded. She wasn't much interested in money.

"She was in her mid-fifties. You've seen pictures of her, Emma. I've always thought she was as handsome as a woman gets—pure Lakota, with cheekbones like knife blades and the high nose of the Indian on the old-time nickel. Her eyes were as black as space and as bright as stars. Our old stories say we used to be star people. I could see that in her eyes, even though she always dressed like a white, and my relatives on Standing Rock said she thought like a white.

"It's hard to pick the worst time for Indians. Was it when we lost our land, not through wars—we Lakota won our wars!—but through treaties? Or was it when we starved on the reservations and were shot down by soldiers and agency police? Or when our children were stolen from us and taken to boarding schools, dressed in white clothing and punished if they spoke their own language?

"I think the worst time was the middle of the 20th century, when our elders died, the ones who had grown up in the old days and learned the old ways from their parents and grandparents. White people had their history in books and movies that showed cowboys shooting down the Indians. Our history was in the minds and mouths of those old men and women. When they died—the last survivors of Little Big Horn and

Wounded Knee, people who had known Sitting Bull and Crazy Horse and seen mammoths wading in the shallows of the Missouri River—then it seemed as if we might vanish as entirely as the mammoths. A few bodies might be left, shambling drunks or white people in red skins, but we would be gone." She paused and drew a deep breath, then got up and went for more iced tea.

We drank in silence for a while. The tea was so cold against my tongue! So tart with lemon and sweet with sugar! The sunbeams that entered the room were almost horizontal now. Dust motes danced in them.

"I think it was in this period that Clara, her daughter and my mother, came to dislike Rosa so much. She would come out to Standing Rock in her Chrysler New Yorker—a big, heavy, burgundy-colored car—climb out and stand in the dirt road, looking tired and remote. It was a long, hard drive from St. Paul, and that may explain her expression. But Clara took it as a disowning.

"Rosa always wore slacks, shirts and comfortable shoes on these trips. Even wrinkled by the long drive to the reservation, her clothing looked expensive; and her comfortable shoes shone under their film of South Dakota dust. To Clara, Rosa was a white woman in a red skin. Living on the reservation, watching the old people die and the young people give in to despair, nothing could be worse to her. Rosa had turned her back on the Lakota, so Clara turned her back on Rosa.

"This was done silently. Rosa had money to give, and Clara's family on the reservation was desperately poor. She took her mother's money, but refused to visit her in St. Paul—a terrifying place!

"Clara married in 1945. Her husband was a soldier from Rosebud, back from the war: Thomas Two Crows. I don't know how they met, only that he was very handsome and full of stories. My relatives on Standing Rock told me that later. Somehow the stories—about Rosebud and his travels as a soldier—tantalized Clara, though she was afraid to visit St. Paul. I don't know why. Maybe because he was a handsome young warrior of proven courage, full of apparent confidence.

"I was born in 1949, the only child that lived, though there had been two before me. Thomas was drinking heavily by then. He died a few years later. He'd been drinking at a friend's house. After a while, they noticed he wasn't there. He must have gone out to pee, my relatives on Standing Rock told me. It was snowing, with a strong wind blowing, and he got lost. They found him two days later, after the storm ended, frozen like one of Rosa's mammoths. If I sound cold when I tell you this, remember that I didn't know him. He died when I was so young. And maybe I'm angry with him for losing himself in drink and the winter. It was a long time ago, and I should have forgiven him by now. But Clara needed him.

"I did know her, though she died when I was still a child. I remember her sitting in our little house, which Thomas paid for with his soldiering money. She was silent for hours at a time. Her anger made the house seem dark to me. It wasn't the darkness of night, with stars blazing above Standing Rock; but the darkness of a winter afternoon when the sky is low and gray, and a cold wind is blowing out of the north. As much as possible, I stayed outside and waited for Rosa's next visit. She came in her big, burgundy-colored car, dust all over the side panels. Once—it must have been in late summer—the entire front of the car was caked with dead grasshoppers. She hated that and spent hours cleaning the grill.

"I'd run to her, and she'd embrace me. She smelled like no other person I knew. Later I discovered it was the scent of fine soap and perfume. There were always gifts for me: wonderful toys, books and her own stories about the Twin Cities of St. Paul and Minneapolis. I gave the toys away. It would have been wrong to keep them, when the children around me had nothing similar. But I kept the books, and I treasured Rosa's stories. The Twin Cities sounded like the Emerald City of Oz to me. I wanted to visit her, and Rosa invited me many times. But Clara wouldn't let me go. She was afraid that Rosa would steal me, the way the white people had stolen so many Lakota children.

"Well," said Grandmother and paused. "This story is about Rosa, not about me.

"She kept at her research, going to the Hill Institute almost every day. The work she did in this period did not lead to any important discoveries. Her real task was making sure that her collection of frozen mammoth tissue remained frozen.

"The mammoths endured nine years longer, the last one—an old male at the Cleveland Zoo—dying in 1957. It was the end of an era, white commentators said. The Old West was gone, along with its most famous denizens. We heard about the death out in the Dakotas and mourned deeply. The sacred mammoths, our allies for generations, were no more. We and the few remaining buffalo were alone in the terrible world made by white men. Our grief was so deep that people died of it. Most were old people, but that was the year that Clara became sick.

"T.B. killed Clara—and bitterness and grief, I have always thought, though she might have lasted longer in a warmer place. That house was cold as well as dark.

What was left for her? The old ways had died, along with her husband and the last mammoth, Trojan. She was losing me to Rosa. She sat in the dark house, in her own darkness, and coughed. Rosa tried to get her good medical care, but Clara wouldn't leave the reservation.

"Rosa came to Standing Rock and sat with her while she was dying, though only at the very end. As long as Clara was conscious, she refused to have Rosa near her. It was a bad situation, and it did not make the other relatives happy. This was not a good way to leave life. But Clara did.

"When she was gone and in the ground, Rosa brought me to St. Paul. I finally made the journey I had wanted to make for years. What a way to make that journey! I sat beside Rosa in her old Chrysler New Yorker, stiff with grief. The fields of eastern South Dakota went past, flat and green and foreign. Trees, which were rare among the golden-brown hills of my home, became common. They didn't remain along the creeks and rivers. Instead, they grew in rows between the fields and in clusters around the farm houses, and—finally, as we reached eastern Minnesota—in woods that covered the hilltops.

"All the people we saw were white, their faces burnt red by summer, their hair brown or blond. They gave us unfriendly looks. 'Don't worry,' said Rosa. 'They may stare, but that's as far as it's likely to go. As a rule, Minnesotans don't say what's on their minds.'

"This didn't reassure me. But we arrived safely in St. Paul. Rosa drove me through streets lined with tall elms and bigger houses than I had ever seen before. The lawns were as green as the Emerald City. Sprinklers flashed in the sunlight like diamonds. I felt utterly lost. Now I began to cry—not for Clara, but for myself.

"'It will be all right,' said Rosa.

"I was still crying when we arrived at her house. I stopped once we were inside, awed by the house's size. Two full stories and three bedrooms! One bedroom would belong to me, Rosa said. The house was old, built more than fifty years before, but Rosa had installed a state of the art bathroom, and a new, electric kitchen. I was entranced and frightened. How could I use objects so clean and shining? Clara had made do with an outhouse and a well.

"There was a television set in the living room. On top of it stood a mammoth family, carved out of honey-colored ivory. It was mammoth ivory from Siberia, Rosa said, thousands of years old. A great curving mammoth tusk hung over the living room fireplace. This came from an animal that had died in the 20th century. 'They lasted so long,' Rosa said sadly. 'If we had managed to keep them alive just a little longer, I am confident that modern science would have found a cure for their illness and a way to keep them in existence indefinitely. Well, their tissue remains, and it is my job to make sure it stays safely in the Institute freezers. There are times, Emma, when the best one can do is preserve.'

"Louis W. Hill had died in 1948, though I didn't learn this until later. His will left a substantial sum to the Hill Institute, but only if the institute continued to maintain Rosa's mammoth remains on its premises in a safely frozen state, with Rosa on staff as the custodian. Of course, there were scientists at the Institute that thought this was folly. They wanted Hill's money, but not the mammoths or Rosa. The rest of her career was a fight to keep her job and the freezers full of mammoth fetuses and tissue. It was as hard as trying to maintain treaty rights. But as I said, I learned this later.

"The house's dining room had two splendid

photographs of mammoths by Ansel Adams. Louis Hill had commissioned him to record the Glacier herd in its last days. Adams was not an animal photographer, but mammoths were part of the west he loved deeply; and they were vanishing. He accepted the commission. Both of Rosa's photographs showed the animals at a distance, grazing in a meadow below tall pines and snow-streaked mountains. Seen with Adams's eye and taken with his box camera, the mammoths seemed as solid and permanent as the landscape they inhabited.

"I came to Rosa's house in the summer of 1958, at the age of nine. By mid-August I was settled into my new room. The windows looked into green caves made of leaves, a disturbing sight for someone used to the wide, treeless distances of western South Dakota. When sunlight shone in, it was tinged green, and green shadows danced on my floor and walls. The days were hot and humid, the nights were full of noise: leaves rustling, bugs singing, radios playing, people talking on neighboring porches. The sky, hedged by rooftops and foliage, held too few stars.

"It was hard, but I survived that first summer. Children are resilient! In the fall I went to school. Rosa managed to get me into the University of Minnesota lab elementary school, though this wasn't easy at short notice. She said I would get a better education and encounter less prejudice. 'Prejudice against Indians is deeply rooted here. But the world is changing. The powers that were defeated in the last world war have shown us how bad human society can become. Maybe we will learn from this and make the world better.'

"Unlike Clara, Rosa was an optimist. It may not be a more rational way to see the world, but it makes life happier.

"She was right about the education I got at U Elementary and U High. It was good. To this day, I don't know how much prejudice I encountered. I was shy and lonely, the only Indian student in a school that was entirely white, except for one African-American family and a single Asian-American student. For the most part the other students were polite and left me on my own. Once or twice, a few were cruel in an ordinary, adolescent way. The other children stopped that behavior. I was not to be a target or a friend.

"You have to remember that I wasn't Indian in an obvious way. My last name was Ivanoff. It was the only thing that Clara got from Sergei, except possibly for Russian sadness. Rosa thought it would be better to use Ivanoff than Two Crows. 'White people are more likely to take you seriously, if you have a white name,' she told me. I could have used Stevens, which was her white name, but I think she wanted that small memento of Sergei.

"My eyes were blue; my hair was brown and wavy; and I was a lot lighter than I am now, because I was so bookish. Either I was inside reading, or I was outside under a tree reading. Sunlight scarcely ever touched me.

"I don't think it was prejudice which kept me alone, though I can't be certain. I think it was my bookishness and inability to understand the other students. What on earth made them tick? Their lives—made of dates and grades—seemed small and confined, like the neighborhoods hemmed in by houses and trees. Their plans seemed equally small: a college education, followed by a good job and marriage. Surely there was more to life than this. I wanted something larger, something as wide as the sky over Standing Rock, though I didn't know what. So I read science fiction and dreamed.

"My one friend was the Asian-American student, Hiram Fong. His sister was retarded; we used that kind of language in those days; and he was his family's hope. They were betting on a sure thing, Rosa told me. 'Hiram is as smart as your grandfather Sergei.'

"How can I describe him? He wasn't shy like me, but he had a cutting wit that scared the other children; and he was far too bright to be popular. Half the time I didn't understand what he was saying. Almost no adolescents in any era understand irony, which was Hiram's favorite kind of humor; and few adolescents of the time understood 20th-century physics, which was his passion. My twin loves were biology and literature, though I wasn't interested in analyzing works of fiction, any more than a fish wants to analyze water. I simply wanted to sink into them and live among words the way a fish lives among underwater plants.

"We both liked science fiction. That was the bond that held us together. And we liked each other's families. Hiram's father was a research doctor at the U. His mother had an advanced degree, I think in psychology, but stayed at home to care for Hiram's sister, a sweet Down's syndrome child, who did far better than such children were expected to do in the 1960s.

"Their house was like Rosa's, large and full of books and artifacts. In the case of the Fong family, the artifacts were from China: silk rugs and porcelain vases, framed examples of calligraphy, opium pipes. Opium was a wonderful medicine, Dr. Fong said, if used prudently and with thought. When shoved down people's throats by the British empire, it was a curse.

"Like Rosa, the Fongs saw a world differently from most of the people I knew, and that made me comfortable with them. Although they didn't like frozen food—Mrs.

Fong always used fresh ingredients when she cooked—they respected the work Rosa had done. 'At present, we have a limited need for frozen tissue,' said Dr. Fong. 'But I'm sure the need will increase, and your grandmother's work will become increasingly important.'

"'Maybe we'll be able to make people someday,' said Hiram as he picked over his dinner with flashing chopsticks. 'Out of frozen parts, like the Frankenstein monster. Or maybe we'll be able to freeze people and wake them a thousand years in the future. That sounds more interesting than frozen peas.'

"'There will probably be more practical uses for the techniques which Rosa Stevens has pioneered,' said Dr. Fong.

"Mrs. Fong, who was a reader, said, 'The monster wasn't made from frozen parts. He might had turned out better if he'd been fresher. Cynthia, please don't play with your food.'

"Hiram and I graduated from high school in 1967. The United States was at war in Asia and at home, against its own citizens. You must have studied this in school, Emma."

"The burning of the cities," I said. "And the Black Panthers and AIM."

"The American Indian Movement came a little later. Otherwise you are correct. Even Minneapolis burned a little in this period. It was a modest blaze, compared to places like Detroit.

"Hiram went to Harvard. I went to a small liberal arts college outside Philadelphia. He and I swore to stay in touch, and we did for our first year. After that, circumstances pulled us apart. Hiram's interest in physics intensified and left him little time for any other interest. I developed an interest in politics. He thought the war was wrong, and he had no desire to go to Vietnam; but he knew he was likely to need a security clearance in order to do his kind of physics. Protesting the war was a risk. He wouldn't take it.

"I felt sorry for him and a little contemptuous. How could anyone be so careful, in that era when everything was being questioned and the world seemed full of possibility?

"The thing your teachers may not have told you is how full of hope the late '60s were. Yes, there was violence. The police and FBI and National Guard were dangerous. Plenty of people—good people—died in fishy ways; and plenty went to prison for things they almost certainly did not do. But the times were changing, and many of us thought we were building a new world in the shell of the old. As it turned out, we were wrong, at least for the time being. The '60s wound down slowly through the '70s, and in 1980 Ronald Reagan began a long period of reaction.

"I still think Hiram was wrong to be careful. We stopped corresponding, because we no longer had anything important to say to one another. Our friendship ended before the war did, not with an argument, but in silence. I was able to track his later career through the science magazines. It was impressive. I have always been surprised that he didn't win a Nobel Prize like Sergei.

"After graduation, I stayed in the east and began work on a Ph.D. in biology. I never got involved with AIM, though I read about it in the papers. The occupation of Alcatraz! The battles on Pine Ridge! Why didn't I come home to St. Paul or Standing Rock? Maybe because I felt more comfortable with political theory than with shoot-outs; and I didn't feel that much like an Indian; and my issue was peace.

"When I came back to St. Paul for visits, I noticed that Rosa was undergoing a strange transformation. Always cold and increasingly indifferent to her appearance, she wrapped herself in cardigans and throws, which made her look like a 19th century Lakota matriarch in a blanket. Her hair, which had always been short and neatly styled, grew long. She wore it in braids wound around her head or hanging down. Her face, wrinkled by age and sunlight, looked like the faces of my great-great-aunts.

"She still went to the Hill Institute daily. Louis W. Hill's will had mentioned no retirement age for her. This outraged the other scientists. By this time the Institute had a director who'd decided—after consulting several lawyers—that the best thing to do was out-wait Rosa. Louis Hill was a man with a passion for control and an eye for detail. He had micromanaged the building of Glacier Park. Even the trim on the famous lodges and the design of their menus had gone past him for approval. Death might cause him to lose control of Glacier. It belonged to the American people, at least in theory. The Institute was his alone. Living or dead, he would control it. His bequest had numerous stipulations; if these were not followed, his money was to go to Glacier for maintenance of the lodges.

"The director could try to break the will, but he was likely to fail. He could ignore the stipulations, but the Department of the Interior had been coveting the Hill money for decades and was likely to sue. Better to put up with Hill's eccentricities: the out-of-date Art Deco building with its tile facade of extinct mammoths and the doddering Indian scientist. Let Rosa potter around her office and lab. In the end, she would die of old age, and the space could be put to better use.

"She lived into her ninety-third year and kept going to work until the last few weeks of her life. When she died—in 1985—I inherited her house.

"As she requested, I had her cremated. She wanted to be buried on Standing Rock. I wasn't sure how my relatives would feel about this, so I didn't tell them what I was going to do. Remember that I had been living in the white world for a long time. I stopped learning how to be Lakota at the age of ten, and there were big gaps in my Lakota education.

"I took Rosa's urn to the reservation and borrowed a horse from my second cousin Billy Horn. By this time, Billy was a middle-aged man with a comfortable gut; but he had been a lean and angry AIM activist with long, flowing hair and a feather tucked into the band of his cowboy hat. His hair was in two braids now. He still wore a cowboy hat, minus the feather; and he still had a rifle—he was one hell of a shot—but he didn't pose with it anymore. Instead, it stayed in his pickup till he needed it. 'Four-legged varmints now,' he told me. 'I gave up shooting at the FBIs. It's a waste of ammunition.'

"The horse Billy loaned me was an appaloosa with an easy gait and beautiful manners. 'It'd be easier to fall out of a rocking chair,' he said. 'Try to stay on board. You don't want to hurt Moonie's feelings.' He stroked the mare's lovely neck.

"I rode into the dry, golden hills. Hawks soared above me in a wide, wide blue sky. These were Swainson hawks, not the Redtails I knew from Minnesota. It came to me as I rode that loved this country. The Missouri was a blue gleam in the distance. One of those damn lakes, made by the damn Corps of Engineers. But from here you couldn't seen the eerie, unnatural pool of water, edged with bare mud flats. Instead, you could imagine the river as it ought to be, full of shoals, edged with willow and cottonwood bottoms. There would be—should be—driftwood floating in the slow, late-summer current, coming to rest on shoals; and mammoths should wade in the shallows, sucking up the muddy water in their trunks and spraying one another.

"I unpacked my shovel and dug Rosa's grave. After I buried her, I burned some sage. Moonie cropped dry grass nearby. That afternoon I decided I'd come back to Standing Rock, though I wasn't sure when. I'd finish my Lakota education.

"I returned to Billy's house at twilight. He took care of Moonie. 'Didn't do her any harm that I can see. Did everything go all right? Did you get Rosa settled?'

"I looked at him with surprise. He grinned. 'You may have a lot more degrees than I do, but that doesn't make me stupid, Liz. It was pretty easy to figure out what you wanted Moonie for. I'm planning to follow your trail tomorrow, go and talk to Rosa and make sure every thing's okay with her.'

"'I wasn't sure I ought to do it.'

"'Crazy Horse said his land was where his dead were buried. That's how we nail all this down.' He waved his hand around at Standing Rock, hidden in darkness. 'So long as we can keep the anthropologists from digging everyone up. If I was going to argue about anything, it'd be the cremation. It isn't traditional. But Rosa always did things her own way.'

"He was joking about the anthropologists. We'd managed to stop them by then and gotten a lot of our ancestors back from places like the Smithsonian. The current problem was people who stole artifacts and fossils from our land. An entire Tyrannosaurus Rex taken and sold to the Field Museum! People have no shame! They will steal *anything* from Indians!"

My grandmother paused and glared, her blue eyes gleaming brightly. Then she took a deep breath and continued her story.

"I went back to St. Paul and looked at Rosa's house. I'd visited her regularly, but it wasn't my home anymore; and there were places—the basement and the attic—where I hadn't been in years.

"The attic looked ordinary: unfinished, full of dust and boxes. I'd have to go through them all, I thought and groaned out loud. The basement was full of freezers. Not the kind you use for storing your Glacier frozen peas. These were the big freezers you'd find in a lab. Heaven knows how she got them down the stairs. Large men and some kind of hoist, I imagined. A note had been taped on one of the freezer doors. 'Dear Liza,' it said in shaky print 'I don't trust the director of the Institute, so have moved my tissue here. There are two backup generators. Please keep the temperature constant. Love, your grandmother.'

"I laughed with surprise, though not with pleasure. Rosa must have gotten stranger than I had realized in her last years. Moving mammoth tissue into her basement? How was I going to sell the house in this condition? I laughed again and shrugged my shoulders, then made sure the freezers were running properly. One thing at the time. First I had to clean the house.

"Some people's lives change dramatically, Emma, in a single moment, through a single decision or event. That has never happened to me. My life has always changed slowly, through a series of small events and decisions.

"I took my first step at Standing Rock, when I realized how much I loved those golden hills. Step two was finding the freezers and making sure they were running properly. Without thinking it through, making no conscious decision, I made the freezers my responsibility. If there is a moral in my story, it's do nothing lightly. I'm not complaining about the way my life turned out. I have enjoyed it so far. But I wish I'd been more mindful in places.

"Step three was cleaning the house. You may think of that as a tiresome project, like cleaning your bedroom. But I was going over my grandmother's life, exploring it the way Lewis and Clark explored the Missouri River and Rocky Mountains. Like them, I found plenty of mammoths; and like them, I did a lot of hard, dirty work. If I had to decide which I'd rather do—clean another house like Rosa's or drag a boat up the Missouri River, I'd have to consider a long time before making my decision.

"The closets were not difficult. Rosa had gotten rid of most of her clothing. The woman I remembered as elegant had spent her last years in blue jeans, flannel shirts, frayed cardigans and battered shoes. Nothing was in good enough condition to give to a homeless shelter. It all went in the trash.

"The boxes in the attic were business papers, most of them years old. It's amazing what otherwise sane people will save! Maybe Rosa became anxious as she aged and afraid of throwing anything out, or maybe she simply became tired of sorting through papers. Almost everything could be burned, which I did on a cold, wet day when rain beat against the living room windows. There is something satisfying about sitting by the fireplace on such a day and watching old tax returns curl and blacken.

"Some of the burden of Rosa's belongings lifted off me that day, though I knew the hardest work still lay ahead. The house was full of books. There was no way I could fit Rosa's collection into my small apartment in Massachusetts; and I didn't want most of the collection. But a book can't be thrown away, and selling it or giving it away has to be done carefully. The best thing is to give books to friends. Rosa's friends were gone by then. She had outlived them all. And none of my friends were in the Twin Cities.

"I planned to keep the books on Indians and packed them for shipment east. Then I went in Rosa's den and looked at the books on mammoths. They lined one wall. Another wall was windows, looking out on Rosa's garden, which had become a wild mixture of perennials and weeds. She had been such a careful gardener in the past! A third wall had her desk and an antique file cabinet made of oak. Two of the drawers were full of articles on mammoths and freeze drying, many written by Rosa. The other two drawers were full of Rosa's notes.

"Surely the contents of the den should go somewhere special. This was Rosa's life work, and she had been a distinguished scholar. I gritted my teeth and called the director of the Hill Institute. I don't remember his name any more. It was something that sounded East Coast and English stock: two last names stuck together with a title in front. Dr. Ramsey Sibley or Crosby Washburn. His accent was midwestern with a trace of East Coast refinement. He was very sorry to hear of my grandmother's death. A remarkable woman! An inspiration to us all! And no, he wasn't interested in her papers. 'We have moved in a new direction here, away from mammoths, Ms. Ivanoff. The university might be interested. I suggest you try them.'

"I mentioned the mammoth tissue. Dr. Sibley chuckled. 'I'm afraid your grandmother became a bit eccentric toward the end. She decided the tissue would be safer in her basement. We didn't oppose her decision. As you may know, Mr. Hill's will required us to keep the tissue in perpetuity. But it belonged to Dr. Stevens; she had the right to remove it. Once it was gone, our lawyers told us, we do not have to take it back.'

"This sounded like shifty law to me, but I wasn't going to argue. I thanked Dr. Crosby Sibley for his help and hung up.

"There I was, Emma, with a den full of mammoth books and a basement full of frozen mammoth. I could pack the den and put it in storage. But the tissue was a serious problem. I couldn't put the house on the market until I found a home for it. I spent the next two weeks desperately calling academic institutions. But it was summer. The people who made decisions were not around.

"I was still sorting and packing. Rosa's sheets and towels were too worn to sell or give away. They went in the trash. The kitchen had a few things I wanted: handmade cups and dishes by local potters. Looking at the rest, I decided on a yard sale.

"At last I reached my childhood room. The elm outside the window was gone, replaced by a silver maple. Otherwise, the room was unchanged. A star quilt covered the bed. One of my cousins on Standing Rock had made it. My favorite stuffed animal, a threadbare mammoth named Mamie, lay on the pillow. One of her glass eyes had been replaced years ago and was blue. Its mate, which was original, was golden brown.

"I had reached some kind of limit. It isn't easy to sort through the belongings of the person who raised you. If I hadn't been so busy, I would have realized that I was sick with grief. In addition, I was frustrated. I couldn't leave the freezers untended; and I wasn't going to be able to find a new home for the tissue before fall. I'd have to ask for a leave of absence from my job. If my department wouldn't give it to me, I'd have to resign.

"That evening I sat in Rosa's living room and drank wine, looking at the objects I hadn't yet packed: the mammoth figurines on top of Rosa's ancient TV, the mammoth tusk over the mantel, Ansel Adams' photographs and most of the books. What was I going to do? Why had Rosa landed me with this mess? Why had she gotten old and died? Didn't she realize how much I would miss her? Even though I hadn't been home often, I had drawn comfort from knowing she was there, pottering around her garden and her tissue. I am an elder now, Emma. But I still miss my own elders, Rosa especially.

"I've never been much of a drinker. It's a bad habit for Indians. But that night I had a glass or two too many. I felt a bit hazy when I went up to bed. Instead of going to the guest bedroom, where I had been staying, I went to my old room. I took the star quilt off the bed and folded it, then lay on the clean sheets, which smelled of lavender. Rosa had loved the stuff. I'd found sachets tucked between her threadbare linens and in every clothing drawer.

"I dozed off, lying next to Mamie, and dreamed. I don't usually remember my dreams, and when I do they are usually fragments of the day's events, fitted together crazily, like a jigsaw puzzle done wrong—evidence that white psychologists are right, when they say our dreams are simply our minds sorting through recent experiences, as part of the process of storing them in our RAM.

"This dream was different. I was in a house built of bones. The only light was a small, dim fire; and shadows filled the house. Nonetheless, I was aware of the bones. They were huge.

"A tiny, withered woman sat across the fire from me. She wore a hide dress, stained by smoke and spotted with grease. It might have been white once. Now it was dun. Her hair fell over her shoulders, long and loose and gray.

"'I don't want this problem,' I said to her. 'Rosa handed it to me after she died. She didn't give me a chance to argue or refuse. I don't belong here. This isn't my life.' I waved around at the house made of bones, though what I really meant was Rosa's house.

"'Don't talk to me of life,' the old woman said. 'My people are dead; and your people are likely to follow. Isn't that the promise which was made to the Lakota? If they respected the mammoths, the buffalo and the Lakota would survive.'

"'The buffalo have survived,' I said.

"'Just barely! How many were left at the end of the Great White Killing? A few hundred! All the thousands alive today are descended from those few. I am a spirit, not a geneticist, but surely the species has gone through a genetic bottleneck. It cannot have the genetic variation it had two centuries ago.'

"'The same would be true of mammoths, if they were brought back,' I said.

"'Rosa saved a lot of tissue, though it did not come from a large number of individuals. It might be possible to find variation among so many chromosomes,' the old woman said. 'We mammoths might be in better shape than the buffalo, if we were alive. We could not be in worse shape than we are now.'

"Another voice spoke from the darkness, 'You have studied biology. You know about the new technologies that are coming into existence. All these white men starting companies to make money out of genes!

The technology we need to re-create our people will be invented soon.'

"Now I saw the second person: a solidly built, middle-aged woman. Her long, braided hair was black; and her dress was the creamy color of clouds on a hot summer afternoon, when they shine through the haze above Standing Rock.

"'Biology is a tricky business,' I said to the second woman. 'You can't listen to the men who start gene tech companies. Of course they promise miracles in the next year or two. They're looking for investors. I have no reason to believe it will possible to re-create mammoths from frozen tissue in the near future.'

"'It won't be possible at all, if the tissue isn't there,' said the crone.

"'There has to be tissue in other places,' I replied.

"A third voice—young and clear and musical—spoke, 'Rosa was *the* great expert on the freezing of mammoths. Has anyone has done work equal to hers? How good are the samples in other places?'

The third woman—slim and graceful, in a hide dress as white as fresh snow—moved out of the shadows. She stopped next to the matron. The crone sat at their feet. They all stared at me, their dark eyes shining in firelight.

"I said, 'I'll find a home for the tissue. I owe Rosa that much. But that will be the end of it. I have my own life to live.' The dark eyes kept watching me. 'Are you sure you are Indian spirits? You know a lot about biology.'

"'First of all,' the crone said, 'We are in your dream. Obviously, we know what you know. And we, like you, are at the end of the 20th century. White people have a god who exists outside time and history and pays far too little attention to his creatures' misbehavior, in my opinion.

"'Indian spirits live in the world we helped make. Why not? We did good work! It's a good place! And like people of every kind—the two legs and four legs, birds and fish and insects—we change in response to time and events. Don't expect us to be like the spirits in an anthropology textbook.'

"'And don't drink so much,' the matron said. 'It isn't good for you.'

"That was the last thing the women said to me. I think they turned into mammoths, and the house vanished, so we were all standing on a wide, dark plain, under a sky packed full of stars. But maybe I made that part up. Maybe I made everything up. I have never been certain about dreams, Emma, though many other people are, and I respect their opinions.

"I woke my old bedroom, next to Mamie. For a while, I lay in the darkness, trying to fix the dream in my memory. Finally, I got up and turned on a light and wrote the dream down. Did I believe I had actually spoken with spirits? No. The dream came from alcohol and my stay in the mammoth-haunted house. Rosa was the person who spoke with mammoths, not I. Still, it had been so vivid and had seemed so full of meaning.

"It was time to tackle the books, I decided. Not Rosa's scholarly collection, but the rest. Her popular science books were out of date; I wasn't interested in modern Russia; and I rarely read novels. Almost everything could go into the yard sale, along with thirty years of *Scientific American* and *National Geographic*.

"I held the sale three weeks later. The day was hot and bright, the sky full of big cumuli that were likely to become thunderclouds by late afternoon. I moved Rosa's belongings onto the front lawn: books and kitchen ware and a few pieces of furniture.

"The first person to arrive was a tall man with long, straight, black hair. It flowed over his shoulders and down his back. He wore a plaid shirt, jeans, work boots and a wide belt with a silver and turquoise buckle. Maybe you don't think I can remember him so clearly after all these years. But I do. Not that it's hard to remember what Delbert wore on any given day. His costume rarely changed. In the winter, his shirts were flannel, and sometimes his belt buckle was beadwork. His brown skin was lightly scarred by acne. His eyes were hazel, though I didn't notice this at first. How could I? He was bent over the books. He was obviously Indian, but not Lakota. Ojibwa, I thought, looking at his broad chest. An academic or a member of AIM or both.

"Other people came and bought furniture and dishes. The man remained with Rosa's books, going through them carefully. Finally, he came over with a stack. They were mostly histories and mostly about Minnesota and the Upper Midwest. 'I was hoping for more on Native Americans,' he said. 'And mammoths. They aren't nearly as important to the Ojibwa as to the Lakota and Dakota, but we do have some mammoth stories and songs.'

"'I'm keeping those,' I said.

"'My tough luck,' he said and smiled. I noticed his eyes. There were white people in his background. Probably voyageurs. 'My name is Delbert Boisvert,' he added. 'You must be Rosa's granddaughter. I saw your name in the obituary. I've been watching for a yard sale, since I learned that she died. I don't rice or sugar like my relatives. But I do hunt and gather books.'

"We ended on my porch, talking and drinking lemonade. Delbert helped people load the furniture and dishes they bought. And he recited a song about mammoths that the famous anthropologist Frances Densmore had written down:

> They are coming.
> They are coming like thunder,
> Oh, my Midé brothers.

"After that, he recited an Ojibwa love poem, also written down by Densmore:

> I thought it was
> A loon.
> It was my lover's
> Splashing oar.

"'Depending on the direction of the canoe—arriving or departing—it's a sad or happy love song,' Delbert said. 'I like happy songs. For me, the canoe is arriving.'

"That's how I met your grandfather. I had always been careful about love before, maybe because I'd lost my mother and home when still young. I had learned that people were not reliable. They would die like Clara or vanish out of my life like my Standing Rock relatives.

"You would think I could have looked at Rosa and seen her reliability. She loved me and cared for me as long as she lived. If I had been paying better attention, I could have learned about integrity and loyalty. Rosa was always herself and always loyal to me.

"In any case, we talked till midnight. Then he went home, and I went to my bedroom. There were no dreams that night, just me staring into darkness and seeing Delbert's male beauty. There's nothing lovelier than a good-looking man. He's like a tom turkey spreading his feathers or a mammoth bull trumpeting.

"Del came back the next morning, and we spent the day talking about my life in St. Paul and Massachusetts and his life on the Red Lake Reservation and in Minneapolis.

"I was partly right about him. He had studied at the University in the studio art department, though he didn't have a degree. 'It cost too much money and time. I didn't have enough of either.' He was a painter, he told me. 'In fact, I am two kinds of painter. I do houses to make a living and pieces of canvas to keep from going crazy.' He knew the AIM people, though he wasn't a member of AIM. 'I have disagreements with them about strategy and personal disagreements as well. But I won't speak about them with disrespect.'

"There was a story there, which he did not tell. In many ways, he was an odd duck, more Indian than I was, but not as Indian as his relatives on Red Lake or in the slums along Franklin Avenue in Minneapolis. In those days, Indians were the poorest people in America, the most badly educated, the sickest and the shortest-lived. Even black people lived longer than we did. But there Delbert and I sat on the porch of Rosa's house, drinking iced tea instead of whiskey or beer, two Indians with enough money to get by and good white educations. But I was haunted by the hills of Standing Rock; and he was haunted by Red Lake's forests; and we were both haunted by our relatives and ancestors.

"As I said before, my life has turned on small events and decisions that I often did not notice at the time. When I came west to close Rosa's house, I was certain that I was going back to Massachusetts."

Grandmother paused. I could tell she was thinking. Two vertical lines had appeared between her eyebrows. "I'm not sure I would have sold the house, even if I had not met Del. It was my childhood home and far closer to Standing Rock than my apartment in the east; and the mammoth tissue was a problem. The more I considered the question, the more I realized I couldn't dump it on the first institution that expressed an interest. It was Rosa's life work, a sacred trust. I had to be sure it was used properly.

"But falling in love with Del made my decision almost easy. He was settled in Minneapolis and not interested in moving east. If I went back to Massachusetts, I would lose him. I was not willing to do this. He was so handsome! I am not sure I should tell you this. Does a granddaughter need to know that her grandmother was a romantic, willing to change her life because she met a beautiful man?

"Mind you, there is nothing wrong with beauty, so long as you have the right standards. The right kind of beauty tells you that your potential mate is strong and healthy, able to produce and maintain a large tail or a pair of enormous tusks. It may tell you that he is intelligent, since intelligence depends—at least in part—on good health. It also depends on education and experience. I am speaking about real intelligence, working intelligence, not the intelligence studied by scientists in labs. Del had good health, a good education and lots of useful experience. He was bright and a fine artist. I don't regret picking him."

I was too young to have an opinion on how to choose a mate, though I was interested in how Grandmother went about it. Grandfather lived in New Mexico now, in a house with a big studio full of paintings. I couldn't tell if he was handsome. To me he looked like Gramps: a tall, thin man in faded jeans and a faded shirt, almost always blue. He wore his gray hair in braids; and there was usually a paint-stained rag tucked in his back pocket.

"In any case, I fell in love. We spent the summer together. In the fall, I went east and packed up my apartment, bringing everything back to St. Paul.

"Del moved into the house while I was gone and finished the attic. Rosa had left it as it came to her: bare wood and dust. He sheetrocked the walls and ceiling, put skylights in facing north and covered the floor with black ceramic tiles. They were easier to clean than wood, he said, and he liked the way they looked.

"It's been decades since I last saw the studio, but if I close my eyes, there it is: light flooding through the skylights, reflecting off the white walls and making the black floor shine. Del's paintings lined the room. At that point, his art was abstract, but I could see the landscapes of northern Minnesota in them: broad, dark, horizontal bands like pine forest edging a lake or river; narrow, vertical lines like the trunks of birches; blues as clear as the winter sky; and reds like a sunrise or an autumn maple.

"I loved that studio and the house and Del. It wasn't a wrong choice I made.

"When I got back, I sent out my résumé and got a job at a local community college, Introductory Biology at first. I found that I liked teaching. I hadn't, as an instructor in the east. My students were older than the kids at a university; and they saw education as a way to get ahead in a world that wasn't getting any easier. I think they saw the hard times coming sooner than I did. Thanks to Rosa, I was middle class and out of touch, the way the middle classes so often are. You'd think being Indian would have helped.

"In any case, my students were serious about learning; and teaching is a pleasure, when the students want to learn. Some of them—a surprising number, it seemed to me—liked learning for its own sake, maybe because it was an unexpected gift. Oh brave new world that has such knowledge in it!" Grandmother smiled.

"The college had no facilities for research. But I had plenty to do. The research could wait." She leaned back and flexed her bony shoulders and sighed. "The next thing I knew, I was pregnant with your mother. I hadn't planned to be; it was a genuine accident, but I knew at once that I was going to keep the baby. I was in my middle thirties. If I was going to have children, it was time to get started. By this time, I knew Del and his family well enough to be confident that his genetic material was good. And too many Indian children had died over the years of poverty and disease and simple killing. Too many had been taken from their families and raised white, like Rosa. Too many lost their parents to illness and alcohol. I wanted this child to live and be raised by her parents."

Grandmother paused and I had a sense she was thinking abut things she might not tell me. Finally she said, "Del was less certain. Artists have trouble settling down. Their art asks too much of them. But we talked it through, and I had help from his family. His mother wanted grandchildren, and he owed a lot to her. She had spotted his ability when he was a child and sent him to live with relatives in the Cities, so he'd be able to go to art museums and buy art supplies. Without her, he might have been—what? Another unemployed fisherman, after the Red Lake tribal fishery closed down?

"His father's mother was on my side as well. Delores. She was an elder, very much respected. Your mother was going to be her first great-grandchild. There was no way she was going to let Del off the hook.

"They all would have preferred an Ojibwa mother, but at least I was Indian. They had worried about Del. He had dated a lot of white women."

"What did Great-grandfather Claud say?" I asked.

"He said, they would help, if Del needed help. 'All the venison and wild rice you can eat, and you know my mother can sew. That baby will have the finest clothes of any baby in the Twin Cities.' He kept his promise. Your mother had clothes that could have gone into a museum, covered with beadwork and trimmed with fur. We put them away in case hard times came, and we needed to sell them.

"The baby was born and named Delores, after her great-grandmother. I had planned to go back to work. But my contract with the college was for a year, and they didn't renew it. The pregnancy had been difficult. I had taken a lot of time off. I suspected this was the reason my contract wasn't renewed, but I couldn't prove it. In any case, losing the job was almost a relief. I didn't bounce back from the pregnancy as quickly as women are supposed to. I needed time to recover; and your mother was so tiny and vulnerable! No more so than any baby, but I couldn't imagine putting someone so small, who could barely move and couldn't speak, in the hands of a stranger. I also could not imagine Del as a stay-at-home father. He'd get interested in what he was painting and not even hear the baby cry. I had some money in the bank, my inheritance from Rosa, not a lot, but enough for a while. I decided to wait before I began to look for another job.

"All this time the mammoth tissue was still in the basement. I suppose I should have been a better custodian, but I had been distracted by moving and teaching and having the baby; and I needed time to think. The tissue might be worth money, and we certainly needed money. But would it be right to sell Rosa's life work? I might be able to use the tissue to find a new job, once I was ready to work. I could tell an interested school, 'If you want the tissue, you have to take me as well.'

"I hadn't been entirely negligent. I'd written letters and made phone calls and given away some of the tissue. That was prudent. You shouldn't keep all your eggs— or any organic material—in one basket. Schools knew about me now. More and more were becoming interested. Biotechnology meant it was going to be possible to analyze mammoth DNA and compare it to the DNA of living elephants. That was the kind of achievement that made the papers and TV news and helped get grants. I didn't have the only mammoth tissue on the planet or in the country; but Rosa had made sure that her tissue— my tissue—was in very good shape. I had the freezers and generators checked on a regular basis, and I paid the electric bill as soon as I got it every month."

Grandmother paused. "Where was I?"

"In St. Paul with my mother," I replied.

"We scraped through a year. I took care of the baby and gave away mammoth tissue. Del moved away from abstraction. Now his paintings showed Indians hunting and fishing and ricing. Partly this was the influence of Patrick DesJarlait, the Ojibwa artist from Red Lake. He was dead by then. But Del had studied his work. Of course he had! The world was not full of Ojibwa painters in those days.

"It was also the influence of our trips north to show little Delores to her relatives. Del came back with sketchbooks full of Claud at work. Your great-grandfather had lost his job when the tribal fishery closed. Now he made his living in the old way, hunting and trapping and ricing and doing some construction. Home repairs, mostly. He was also good at fixing cars. On a reservation full of rez cars, this was a valuable skill. Mostly, he got paid in food or thank yous. If you wanted to know poor in those days, you went to a reservation.

"There were sketches of Del's mother holding the baby and old Delores bent over her sewing. Sometimes, when he painted, the figures remained modern Indians; and sometimes their clothes became traditional. There was one I loved—Claud, dressed like an old-time warrior, bent under the hood of a beat-up rez car, working on the engine. I could see the influence of DesJarlait and the WPA or maybe it was the Mexican muralists. Claud in his buckskin and fur and feathers looked like a heroic worker in a post office mural. He was big and bold and bright.

"Del had a show at the American Indian Center in Minneapolis. Then he got a job at the new casino being built south of the Twin Cities. There was a tiny reservation there: Prairie Lake, and this was the end of the 1980s, after the Supreme Court ruled that states could not regulate Indian gaming. It was the start of good times for a handful of Indian bands, the ones near white centers of population. Most, of course, were in the middle of nowhere and did far less well with gaming. But it was a help. I will not be cynical about it. We had been so poor for so long. Even a little money was wealth; and for a few bands, like the ones at Prairie Lake, the money was serious, even by white standards.

"The band decided to name their casino Mammoth Treasure. I suppose it was a good name. Their emblem was a golden mammoth, a male with huge twisting tusks. They wanted a mural in the entrance lobby, showing traditional Indian activities. Del's work fit the bill. Even though he was Ojibwa, and they weren't, he got the job.

"I went down to Prairie Lake with him sometimes. The lobby was circular, and the mural went all the way around the curving wall. If you stood in the middle of the lobby, you were surrounded by a nineteenth century landscape, rolling prairie with clumps of trees. It was a cloudless day in mid-autumn. The grass was tan and gold. The trees were red and brown. In the foreground were Indian hunters on horseback. In the middle distance bison grazed; and in the far distance were four groups of mammoths, one on each side of the lobby, in each of the four directions. Birds sailed above the prairie, so high up that their markings were invisible. But the length of their wings said they were eagles. Hard to say what they were doing there. Bald eagles are fishers and usually keep close to water. The raptors over a prairie ought to be hawks.

"Was the mural corny? Yes. But Del had a streak of romance that went right through him, along with a streak of irony; and the band building the casino absolutely loved the mural; and we needed the money.

"Of course, most of the time when I went down, I saw white plaster and scaffolding. The mural was a work in progress. I nursed little Delores and watched Del or talked with the band treasurer, who was a woman, a big matron with gray hair. The first dribbles of gambling money had gotten her a fine set of new teeth, but it couldn't do anything about the lines in her face. Marion Forte. A good name. She was as strong and solid as a fort. She took to me once she discovered I was Lakota. 'I have nothing against the Ojibwa,' she told me. 'Even though they used to be our enemies. But the Lakota are our cousins. How did you manage to marry an Ojibwa?'

"I told her I wasn't sure. It simply happened. She nodded. 'That's possible. He is a good painter, even though those eagles shouldn't be up there. We aren't close enough to the Mississippi. And those hunters are overdressed, unless they're going to war. All that paint and feathers! No one hunted bison that way.'

"I told her I had wondered about that, and she laughed. 'Most of the council are men. They wanted to see warriors, but they didn't want people to come in and see a war. This is a place to have fun. We can't have blood in the lobby.'

"She was an easy woman to talk to, about the age my mother would have been, if she had lived, and both sharp and kind. So I told her about Clara and Rosa and my childhood and my current life. In the end—it was inevitable—I told her about the freezers in the basement, and the tissue which was an inheritance and problem.

"Marion looked thoughtful. 'Mammoths,' she said. 'No wonder Del has painted them. He's living with what's left of them.' That was the end of the conversation." My grandmother looked at me. "But you must know the next part of the story."

I nodded. "She went to the council and said, they should put money into research."

"Yes," said Grandmother. "And they refused. They were too new to having money. They wanted it for themselves and rest of the band and for the casino, so they could make more money."

"'Men never think ahead,' Marion said. 'That's why they make good warriors. The council president came back from Korea with a chest full of medals. He has never looked beyond the next hill in his entire life. Well, this hill is the new casino. Let's wait and see what lies on the other side.'

"I went home and looked at the bank balance and sent out my résumé. Del was getting paid well for the mural, but that money wouldn't last; and our utility bills were high."

Grandmother shrugged. "Why make a long story longer than it is by nature? The Prairie Lake council voted to set up a foundation. It took another four years, with Marion pushing at every meeting; but it finally happened. By then Del had a job teaching at the Minneapolis College of Art, and he'd even had a show in a white museum—not his current work, but the older abstractions. Young Delores was old enough for day care, though she didn't like it. How your mother yelled the first time I left her!

"The University got the first grant for mammoth research; and I went to work for the research lab. The U had no choice. I came with the money and the mammoth tissue. Did I feel guilty, using the tissue and the Prairie Lake band's clout? Not a bit. It was the 1990s by then, the last great hurrah of capitalism before the dark days of the early 21st century. The white people were busy grabbing everything they could with both hands. I thought, I could do a little of the same, enough to pay the bills and get myself back into research.

"Of course the people in the lab resented me, a woman and an Indian, who had gotten her job through luck and casino money. How could I be any good? I won't bother you with the story of my struggles. This story is about the mammoths, not me. But always remember that power concedes nothing without a demand. It never did, and it never will. 'If there is no struggle there is no progress. Those who profess to favor freedom and yet depreciate agitation...want crops without plowing up the ground, they want rain without thunder and lightening. They want the ocean without the awful roar of its many waters…'"

At the time I did not recognize the quote. It was Frederick Douglass, of course. Odd to hear my grandmother talk about the ocean on the bone-dry Dakota prairie.

"The first several grants came from Prairie Lake. Then other money began to come in, as the lab reported its first success, which was decoding mammoth and elephant DNA and finding out that mammoths were closely related to Asian elephants. The next step was obvious, though not easy: building a viable mammoth egg and implanting it in an elephant." Grandmother smiled. "Imagine what a statement that is! It used to be, we could not imagine re-creating extinct animals, except maybe in science fiction stories. Now we have the quagga—the real quagga, not the bred-back version; and the giant ground sloth, though I'm not sure what use it is, except as an exhibit in a zoo. And we have two species of mammoths, though the Siberian species is a genetic patchwork. Still, it's different enough from our Missouri mammoths to be called a separate species.

"I have to say, my contribution to the research was not key; and I did my own best work later in another area. But I still remember—how could I ever forget?—the morning when the first baby mammoth was born and helped to stand by a vet and the surrogate mother's mahout. The rest of us watched on a monitor. The calf was tiny, unsteady, wet and very hairy. The mother fondled it with her trunk, unsurprised—as far as we could tell—by all the hair.

"The first species brought back from extinction! Not from the edge of extinction, but from the void beyond the edge! The research team broke out champagne, and the Prairie Lake band ordered new commercials for their casino starring the baby. That led to a fight, but the band had good lawyers, and the grants had been carefully written. Prairie Lake owned the right to publicize any results of the research they funded. My colleagues at the U made angry jokes about Indian givers. But the band never asked for its money back. It simply wanted its share of the results, which included—ultimately— enough mammoths to start their own herd. Always be careful what you sign, Emma."

She stopped and leaned back, her eyes closed. It was a long story. Of course, I felt pride. My family had helped save the Missouri mammoths, though most of the mammoths lived north and west of us. The great river was diminishing, due to lack of snow in the Rockies; and the moist bottom lands the mammoths needed no longer existed.

"There's one good side to that," Grandmother said. "They blew up the Oahe Dam. That damn lake is gone. It never looked natural, and it took so much of our land. Though it didn't do to us what it did to the Mandan and Hidatsa and Akikawa. They lost their entire reservation. I know it happened in another century, and I know that people shouldn't hold grudges. Life has gotten better for us and many people. But I hated that lake. I could dance on the dry land where it used to be. In fact I do. That's where we hold the annual Standing Rock powwow."

She didn't say 'powwow.' She said 'wacipi,' which is the Lakota word. But I knew what she meant.

"It would have happened, anyway," Grandmother said. "They would have built mammoths from other DNA. Rosa wasn't the only person who kept tissue, though hers was the best. So don't feel too proud, young Miss Emma. History is a collaborative process. The important thing is to be a part of history and on the right side, which is not always easy to determine. It's not enough to hold onto the past, though we Indians proved that losing the past is dangerous. We almost died of trying to be white. Not that white people have done much better. They almost destroyed the planet by getting and spending and laying waste.

"What do we keep from the past? What do we discard? How do we change? These are all important questions, which all of us have to answer. The mammoths are important, though they may not graze by the Missouri again in our lifetimes. But the bison are back—over a million; and the herds are still growing; and you can see them here on Standing Rock. There's plenty left to do to remake the planet, but we have achieved a fair amount already. One step forward and two steps back, and then one or two or three steps forward. We dance into the future like dancers in a Grand Entry."

At the end of every visit, I went home, rocking through Standing Rock past the grazing bison. My mother's second cousin Thelma in Minot gave me dinner and a bed. In the morning, I rode the eastbound rocket train. Windmills turned. The train glided through forest. My parents waited on the platform in Minneapolis. If I wanted to see mammoths, I could go to Mammoth Treasure Park by the casino. They were there, wading in an artificial river and spraying each other with water, their ancient eyes glittering with pleasure. Above them in the blue sky might be eagles. They have grown so common that they are everywhere these days.

WRITING SCIENCE FICTION DURING WORLD WAR THREE

This essay began as a guest of honor speech, which I gave at Wiscon in 2004. I updated it a year later when the speech was published in *Ordinary People*, a collection of my writing. I am updating it again, because history keeps happening.

I'm going to start with some ideas from Immanuel Wallerstein, a sociologist who has clearly been influenced by Marxism, though I don't know if he would call himself a Marxist.[1]

According to Wallerstein, we are living within a political and economic system which originated in Europe about five hundred years ago but is now worldwide. Politically this system is characterized by nation states. Its economic form is capitalism.

Wallerstein believes this world system is now in crisis, a crisis from which it will not recover. I'm not sure I entirely agree with his reasons for the economic crisis, though I do agree that capitalism is in trouble.

What I find interesting is Wallerstein's analysis of what's happening to nation states.

First, he argues that capitalism—for all that capitalist thinkers thunder against government interference—*needs* national governments. Nation states provide capitalists with protection in the form of patents, copyrights, tariffs and armies. They create an infrastructure which capitalists may not want to build themselves, but are happy to use. Examples in the U.S. are the railroads, funded by huge government land grants; the interstate highway system, built during the Cold War with tax money; and the Mississippi River, which the Army Corps of Engineers has turned into a barge canal. I have spent my life on the Mississippi. A lot of freight gets moved along it and through the St. Lawrence Seaway, another government project.

Nation states fund R&D, turning the results over to manufacturers under cost or for free. They funnel large amounts of money into specific industries, such as war industries. And they control what were called in the 19th century 'the dangerous classes'—poor and working people. Part of this control is direct, through cops and prisons. But the so-called advanced or western nations also provide services—education, health care, pensions—which make life more tolerable and citizens less desperate.

Finally, nation states provide hope, which Wallerstein argues may be their most effective form of control. For more than two hundred years, since the English and American and French revolutions, people have seen the possibility of using national governments to improve their lives, sometimes through revolution, more often through the expansion of suffrage, the creation of political coalitions and the making of laws.

This era—when people hoped to make a better future by gaining control of the state through election or revolution—ended in the late 20th century, according to Wallerstein. By this time, Russia and China had demonstrated that 'Communist' states did not provide people with peace, justice and freedom.[2] The Social Democratic states of Western Europe demonstrated that elected socialists were unable to deliver on the promises of socialism. And the postcolonial states of Asia, Africa and Latin America failed to achieve humane postcolonial societies. Nations of every kind remained enmeshed in a world system dominated by capitalism's drive to accumulate wealth, no matter what the cost to humanity and the planet. My own private image of capitalism and capitalists is the great white shark—a primitive animal, in many ways limited, but very good at what it does. One cannot build a humane society on a base of great white sharks.[3]

According to Wallerstein, because the world system of nation states has failed to deliver a decent life for most people, it has lost credibility. People no longer see the state as a tool to be used to improve human existence.

For him, the key year is 1968, when there were revolutions in France and Czechoslovakia, a brutally suppressed student uprising in Mexico, and violent struggles against war and racism in the U.S. The late '60s is when the American cities burned. If you're too young to remember or weren't living in a burning city, I recommend *Dhalgren* by Samuel R. Delany, a terrific portrait of big American cities in the late '60s. Detroit in 1968 and '69 was exactly like *Dhalgren*. Even the poets were the same.

France, Czechoslovakia, Mexico and America are the struggles I know about. Wallerstein says there were others worldwide. According to him, these were not efforts to seize the state, but struggles against the state, against all states and the very idea of states.

He's arguing that ideas have power. As long as people believe in the state as something worth having, they will work to maintain a state apparatus. At the very least, they will obey laws. When they give the state up as hopeless and useless, its ability to survive is threatened.

One example of this is the collapse of the Soviet Union and the eastern block. The second most powerful nation on Earth simply fell apart, with remarkably little violence for a change so huge.

Another example may be the U.S., where the Bush Administration did its best to dismantle large parts of the federal government. This isn't being done accidentally. Grover Norquist, a conservative thinker and mentor for the Bush Administration, has said that he wants to weaken the federal government until it can be dragged into the bathroom and drowned in the bathtub. Pat Robertson has advocated nuking the U.S. State Department. These people aren't kidding. Their language may be colorful, but they mean what they say.

Why is the American right bent on destroying the federal government, if capitalism needs nation states? Short term, they will be rid of many tiresome government regulations, and the opportunities for stealing of publicly owned resources will be huge. Long term—I suspect Pat Robertson is already working on plans for a new Christian government to succeed the US of A.[4]

If Wallerstein is right, the next fifty years of human history will be a period of breakdown and chaos. It won't be a comfortable period. It's likely to be dangerous. It's also likely to be full of possibility. A stable system is almost impossible to change, according to Wallerstein. Huge efforts produce very small results. The system always tends to re-stabilize. But when a system is breaking down and off-balance, a small effort can create large changes. I think Wallerstein is influenced by chaos theory here, and the gentle flapping you hear in the background is the famous Amazonian butterfly.

The end of the crisis is not certain. The new society which emerges may be as bad or worse than the one we live in now. The kind of theocracy described in *Native Tongue* and *The Handmaid's Tale* seems much more possible to me than it did a few years ago. But if we think and act—we in general, the human race—we may be able to create a new society that is genuinely decent. According to Wallerstein, *now* is the time to think about what kind of society we want to emerge from chaos—and what we are going to do to create that new society.

I am going to move now to the ideas of William S. Lind, Director of the Center for Cultural Conservatism at the Free Congress Foundation. As his title suggests, Lind is a conservative. I suspect he and I don't have a lot in common. But he has some interesting things to say about modern warfare.

He divides modern war into four generations, beginning in the mid-17th century in Europe. I'm going to skip the first three generations, except to say that in all three wars were fought by conventional armies, employed by and controlled by nation states.

Fourth Generation warfare is radically different. In some ways, it is guerrilla warfare, but unlike the American Revolution—an early example of a modern guerrilla war—Fourth Generation warfare is not controlled by a state. It is decentralized, carried on by what might be called non-governmental organizations. At times, as in Iraq (and now Afghanistan), the organization is so loose that one isn't sure an organization exists.

At this point, I'm going to quote Lind. "All over the world, state militaries find themselves fighting non-state opponents... Almost everywhere, the state is losing...

> At (the) core of (Fourth Generation warfare) lies a universal crisis of the legitimacy of the state, and that crisis means many countries will evolve Fourth Generation war on their soil. America, with a closed political system... and a poisonous ideology of 'multiculturalism' is a prime candidate for the homegrown variety of Fourth Generation war.[5]

I don't agree with Lind that multiculturalism is poisonous. But I agree with him that the collapse of the official, white, Christian, flag-waving, Indian-killing, Fourth-of-July American culture is dangerous to the status quo. That culture is what makes all of us—the oppressors and the oppressed—a single, unified nation. It legitimates our government and our economic system.

Now for another quote. It's from an essay by Prince El Hassan bin Talal of Jordan, which appeared in the *Toronto Globe and Mail* on April 7, 2004:

> There are more than forty so-called low-intensity conflicts in the world today. Maybe it is not the Third World War if you are living in Manchester or Stockholm, but if I were living in Madrid when in the bombs at the station went off, it would seem very much like the Third World War to me.

As soon as I read this, I thought, "Yes. The prince is right. We *are* living in the middle of the Third World War."

To sum up, if these three very different men are correct, the near future is likely to be a period of collapsing governmental structures and warfare so widely spread that it can be called a World War. Much that is bad may result from this era of collapse and violence: the rise to power of right-wing religious movements, the reversion to a world comprised of tribes and tribal loyalties. The position of women may well worsen. We've already seen ethnic cleansing in the former Yugoslavia, genocide in Rwanda and something between ethnic cleansing and genocide in Palestine.

Is there a bright side to this dark vision of the future? Do I see hope anywhere? Yes.

Political and social struggles worldwide—struggles I would call progressive—are increasingly aware of one another and connected, via the mass media and the Internet. I'm going to talk briefly about a few of these struggles, starting with the Zapatista Liberation Army. This is an organization of desperately poor Native American farmers, living in the mountains of Chiapas in southern Mexico. It emerged into public view on January 1, 1994—the same day that the North American Free Trade Agreement took effect. From the start, the Zapatistas have addressed themselves to the world. Their remarkable PR man, Subcomandante Marcos, appears to have spent the past ten years in the Mexican jungle, armed with a computer, modem and satellite disk. His manifestoes are wonderfully eloquent, clever and funny. For example:

> A new lie is being sold to us as history. The lie of the defeat of hope, the lie of the defeat of dignity, the lie of the defeat of humanity... In place of humanity, they offer us the stock market index. In place of dignity, they offer us the globalization of misery. In place of hope, they offer us emptiness. In

place of life, they offer us an International of Terror. Against the International of Terror... we must raise an International of Hope. Unity, beyond borders, languages, colors, cultures, sexes, strategies and thoughts, of all those who prefer a living humanity. The International of Hope. Not the bureaucracy of hope, not an image inverse to, and thus similar to, what is annihilating us. Not power with a new sign or new clothes. A flower, yes, (the) flower of hope.[6]

There's a rumor that Marcos has an advanced degree in mass communications. The university that trained him ought to advertise: "You too can charm and amaze the world."

Starting in 1999, internationally organized demonstrations protesting globalization have occurred at almost every meeting of the World Trade Organization.

Globalization is a slippery and dishonest word. It has nothing to do with internationalism; it is an attempt to remove national and local barriers to the movement of capital, and national and local limitations to the power of capital. This includes laws protecting the environment, natural resources and workers. If the WTO has its way, nothing will be safe from the sharks.

The first demonstration—the Battle in Seattle in 1999—shut down the WTO's Third Ministerial Meeting. The ministers simply could not go on. Since then, WTO meetings in Prague, Genoa, Montreal, and Cancun have been met with demonstrations made up of labor union members, farmers, environmentalists, students and indigenous people from all over the world. The most powerful people on Earth meet to divide the Earth up, and they can't do it unless they hunker down behind a wall of cops, concrete and razor wire. There is no place on Earth where the rich and powerful are truly safe.

The 2003 meeting in Cancun ended in failure, due to a rebellion of Southern Hemisphere nations, led by President Luiz Inácio Lula da Silva of Brazil. As far as I can tell from news reports, the demonstrations— and especially the protest-suicide of one of the demonstrators, a South Korean farmer—helped the southern-hemisphere representatives hold firm.

The future of the WTO is currently uncertain.[7]

We now come to the Invasion of Iraq and the worldwide peace demonstration held just before the Invasion. This was an amazing event. Something like ten million people marched in Europe, Asia, Africa and the Americas. The U.S. coverage was not good, so I read Internet editions of English, French, Cuban, and Mexican papers. There were demonstrations in Malaysia, Bangladesh, India, the Middle East, most Latin American countries, and I no longer remember which countries in Africa—all acting in concert, all aware of one another.

I will end this catalog of resistance with a simple observation. Whenever people demonstrate anywhere about anything, some of their signs are in English. People no longer speak only to their locality or nation. They address the entire world.

Do I have any idea where this new international consciousness will lead? Or whether the current international struggles for peace and against capital will produce a better world? No, of course not. I am simply indicating that—as the chief defenses of the old society, nation states and national armies, lose power—a loose, worldwide organization is taking form. It has a decentralized structure and is run from the bottom up. It may represent a new kind of social structure, or it may be a dead end. I have no idea how it will develop or if it will develop at all.

The world is still full of nuclear weapons. AIDS is killing much of Africa and spreading through the former Soviet Union, along with multi-drug-resistant TB. We are running out of fresh water. Our soil is degrading. Hundreds of millions of people live in dire poverty, at the edge of starvation. Right now, the starvation is due to poverty, not absolute lack of food worldwide. But Earth's farmers have not produced enough food to feed humanity for the past four years. We've been making up the difference with stockpiled food. This cannot continue indefinitely or for long.

Petroleum production may be peaking right now, at a time when the demand for oil and gas is rising worldwide. In 2004 Royal Dutch Shell wrote down its petroleum reserves.[8] The company had been lying about how much oil it had. Who else may be lying? I read one expert who has doubts about the Saudi oil reserves.

I haven't even gotten to the Greenhouse Effect.

We are living in an age of revolution *and* in a science fiction disaster novel. No, we are living in several science fiction disaster novels at once. The stakes are huge. Human civilization may be at risk. The solutions are going to require science and technology, as well as political and social struggle.

What are we—as science fiction readers and writers—doing about this? Historically, science fiction has been about big problems, use and misuse of technology, the broad sweep of history and every kind of change. Historically, it has been a cautionary and visionary art form. Are we continuing this tradition? Are we writing books that accurately reflect our current amazing and horrifying age? Are we talking about the kind of future we want to see and how to begin creating it?

Or are we, in the immortal words of the preacher in *Blazing Saddles*, just jerking off?

○ ○ ○

The above, with a few minor changes, is the speech I gave in May, 2004. I want to add a brief update, then move on to some new topics.

In 2005, the Millennium Ecosystem Synthesis Report was released. According to the report, 60 percent of the world's ecosystems are being degraded or used unsustainably, leading to the increasing likelihood of abrupt changes that affect human well-being. Among these changes are new diseases, sudden changes in water quality, creation of dead zones along coasts, collapse of fisheries and shifts in regional climate.

In a world barely able to feed itself now, environmental degradation is scary; and terms such as "abrupt" and "sudden" change are also scary.

It's hard to be sure how severe the impending shortage of oil is, because the estimates of oil reserves cannot be trusted. Per a recent article in *The Guardian*:

> The world is much closer to running out of oil than official estimates admit, according to a whistleblower at the International Energy Agency who claims it has been deliberately underplaying a looming shortage for fear of triggering panic buying.
> The senor official claims the US has played an influential role in encouraging the watchdog to underplay the rate of decline from existing oil fields while overplaying the chances of finding new reserves.[9]

Petroleum powers our current world civilization, which is an obvious statement, but also true. It is key to transportation, agriculture and much industrial production, both as a source of power and as a raw material. It's also a major pollutant, and we need to move on to new energy sources. But it would be nice to make a smooth transition. Right now, it seems as if a major response by world governments is lying and resource wars. Can anyone think of a reason for the U.S. to be in Iraq and Afghanistan, except Middle Eastern and Central Asian oil and gas?[10]

Most disturbing, global warming is happening more rapidly than predicted. The environmental, social and political consequences of climate change will be huge. The American Pentagon is now doing global warming war games. As rivers dry and farmland is lost to drought, there will be wars over scarce resources.

Which brings us back to Prince El Hassan bin Talal. In 2004, he said there were forty low-intensity conflicts in the world. A chart in the September 12, 2009 issue of *New Scientist* puts the number of conflicts worldwide in 2008 at a little under 350. I assume the prince and the magazine are using different definitions of conflict.

For the most part, these are civil wars and guerrilla wars, fought within nations and against national governments. So far as I know, the only conventional armies in operation are the U.S. and its allies, who are fighting Fourth Generation guerrillas in wars that cannot be won, according to William S. Lind.

This is a lot of conflict, and it's occurring throughout the world. I think the prince is correct when he says we are living in the middle of a world war. This war has many apparent causes, but it seems likely that a basic issue is control of resources—food, water, arable land, mineral wealth, forests—and another basic issue is the right to self-determination. Do the billions of poor people on Earth have the right to run their own lives? Do they have the right to enough resources to stay alive and be comfortable?

There is a final problem, which was not evident to me when I gave the speech. The Bush era 'economic boom' was always odd, since it was based on asset inflation, rather than on increased production, higher employment and higher wages. But it looked good to many Americans, so long as they had houses that were growing in value.

The real estate bubble began to deflate in 2006, which led to the collapse of the American (and world) financial bubble in 2008. For a while, *per* respected orthodox economists such as Paul Krugman, the world economy was on the edge of another Great Depression. This was prevented by the US government, which poured more than a trillion dollars into walking dead Wall Street banks. The banks have survived thus far and are once again giving their senior staff gigantic bonuses.

But the underlying economy continues its slow slide. The official—U3—measure of American unemployment was over 10 percent at the end of 2009. U6 unemployment, which includes people who given up looking for work or taken part time jobs out of desperation, was at least 17 percent. One American worker in six is unemployed or under-employed.

Home mortgage foreclosures continue to rise. The commercial real estate market is in trouble, and it's expected that the failure of commercial real estate loans will lead to more bank failures.

This is not a local problem. Prior to the meltdown, much of the world economy depended on American consumer spending, which was funded by a combination of the housing bubble and credit card debt. This has ended.

I don't want to spend a lot of time on the Great Recession, as it is being called. But I want to make a couple of points. (1) We are facing a huge environmental crisis and a planet which may well have more people than it can feed. (2) At the same time, our financial resources have been sucked first into a gigantic bubble and now into an effort to fix the bubble. This effort has focused on saving Wall Street banks, rather than people.

Capitalism has always been subject to booms and busts. In the past, bubbles tended to come at the end of a boom, when investors had gotten too exuberant. Now, the bubbles are appearing more and more frequently, getting larger and bursting in more dramatic and scary ways. More and more resources go into speculation, into the casino economy, rather than into rebuilding the world.[11]

Over the past two decades, there has been a major economic crisis every two or three years: the U.S. stock market crash of 1987; the American savings and loan collapse of the late 1980s and early 1990s; the collapse of the Japanese real estate bubble in 1990, leading to Japan's so-called 'lost decade;' various crises in Latin America in the 1990s, the most dramatic being Argentina and Mexico; the East Asian financial meltdown in 1997; the Russian crisis in 1998; the failure of the Long Term Capital Management hedge fund in the U.S. in 1998, due in large part to the Russian financial collapse; the collapse of the dot com bubble in 2000; the collapse of the U.S. real estate bubble, which began in 2006; and the current Wall Street bank collapse, which began in 2008.

This is a lot of collapsing. It does not look as if we have a stable economic system. The current rescue of

Wall Street seems to be creating a new bubble, since the banks need to do something with the money they have been given, and the easiest thing to do is speculate. This will most likely lead to another financial crisis in two or three years.

This may well be the worst problem we are facing right now: our inability to allocate resources of every kind to where they are needed, if human civilization is going to survive; and our reliance on an economic system that seems unable to do anything except blow bubbles.

I should also note the fantastic waste of capitalist production. In a world at the edge of environmental collapse, we are putting our resources into consumer crap from China, much of which is bought on impulse, then thrown away. We could be building windmills and energy efficient buildings, solar stoves, desalinization plants, and—my favorite—giant space parasols to reduce the amount of sunlight getting to Earth. This last will make the solar stoves less efficient, but they ought to still work; and the parasols would be—in every sense—cool.

So far the world's governments have not done a good job of dealing with global warming or environmental degradation or peak oil. This is especially true of First World governments. The U.S. in particular seems to be dragging its feet and trying to maintain business as usual in the face of an abyss.

This brings us to the struggle against business as usual. One part of the struggle is international movements for peace and a green planet. Another part is liberation movements at the national level.

In Venezuela, Hugo Chávez—a democratically elected, populist president—has been engaged in a multiyear struggle to keep his job. A *coup d'état* in April

2002 failed when hundreds of thousands of Venezuelans demonstrated in support of Chávez; he was returned to power after forty-eight hours.

In December 2002 the management of the Venezuelan state oil company staged a lockout and shutdown, demanding that Chávez resign. This 'general strike' against Chávez did not spread beyond the largely white upper and middle classes and ended in failure. Chávez fired the oil company managers.

The opposition then began collecting signatures for a referendum on Chávez. In 2004 he won the referendum and was confirmed in office. At this point (2010), he has won two elections and six referenda. His position is not entirely secure, given the hostility of the U.S. government. But for the time being, he is proceeding as he promised: to use the oil wealth of Venezuela for the benefit of ordinary Venezuelans, who are desperately poor people of mostly Native American and African descent.

Chávez is currently working—with Cuba, Bolivia and other Latin American countries—to create international trade and banking organizations for Latin America that will replace organizations dominated by the U.S. In theory, these organizations—ALBA and the Bank of the South, among others—will be committed to social progress and the welfare of ordinary people, rather than corporate interests.

In 2003, massive demonstrations, work stoppages and transportation blockages forced President Gonzalo Sánchez de Lozada in Bolivia to resign and flee to the United States. The key issue was privatization of water, oil and gas and the proposed construction of a pipeline. The pipeline would take Bolivian natural gas to Chile, where it would be shipped to California. The Bolivian people would lose a valuable natural resource that could be used to develop their desperately poor country; and—thanks to privatization—their government would not get a fair price for the gas.[12]

Bolivians had seen this before. Starting in the sixteenth century, a huge fortune in silver and tin was taken out of Bolivia, leaving the native population with nothing.[13] The Bolivians did not want to lose another fortune. They took to the streets. In 2005, they forced out President Carlos Mesa, who had succeeded Sánchez de Lozada, and elected Evo Morales, the first Native American president in Bolivian history. The Morales government has renationalized Bolivia's petrochemical resources and drafted a new constitution, giving more power to the indigenous majority. The constitution was voted into effect early in 2009.

Increased natural gas royalties are being used for pensions, support for families with children in school, and no-interest loans to farmers.

Between 1995 and 2005, popular movements in Ecuador toppled seven presidents.[14] The current president Raphael Correa has promised changes and come through on some of his promises, which may mean he will keep his job. A new constitution was approved by popular vote in 2008. The constitution guarantees the right to clean water, universal health care, pensions, and free state-run education through the university level. It also includes a bill of rights for Nature, including the right for Nature to be free of exploitation and environmental harm. Consider how amazing this is: the people of Ecuador have recognized the rights of forests and rivers.

Latin America is especially interesting right now. However, there is a comparable struggle going on in Nepal, involving mass demonstrations, general strikes, and the Unified Communist Party of Nepal (Maoist), which fought a ten-year guerilla war against the royal government, then laid down its arms and won a democratic election. The ruling coalition, which included the UCPN (M), resigned in 2009 after failing to exert civilian control of the Nepalese military; and the UCPN (M) is currently involved in a popular movement against the minority government, which has close ties to the U.S.-advised Nepalese military.

I don't know enough about the UCPN (M) to say if they have a vanguardist political philosophy, but they certainly were a guerrilla army. At the moment, they have changed their strategy to mass action and democratic elections, both of which seem more effective. As the fantasy writer Terry Pratchett likes to say, maybe the leopard *can* change his shorts.

Three things should be noted about these struggles. (1) They are largely nonviolent. (2) Instead of a vanguard party or guerilla army, they involve mass demonstrations, work stoppages, barricades on roads, and elections. (3) There are recurring issues: the right to honest elections, popular control of natural resources, and the right of ordinary people to stay alive. In addition, these movements have all aimed at control of the state.[15]

How does the last fit with Immanuel Wallerstein's theory that governments have lost credibility?

I have gone back and forth with this question, since I find Wallerstein's arguments convincing in many ways. Yet we are seeing popular movements in Latin America that clearly see government as useful, something worth getting and holding.

Part of the answer is—none of these struggles have been single events. Rather, they have gone on for years. The Venezuelans hit the bricks time after time to save the Chávez government. The Bolivians tossed out two presidents; popular leaders and ordinary people have told Morales he has better come through on his promises, or he will be out too.[16] The Ecuadorians have tossed out seven presidents, for heaven's sake. The Nepalese brought down the royal government in 2006 and are now working to bring down another government.

This suggests that the people of these countries see government as a tool or weapon, the best they have available at the moment. If a tool works, we keep it. If it doesn't work, we fix it or toss it. It is not a source of authority or legitimacy.

In addition, I am not at all sure that these popular governments are nation-states in the traditional sense. Rather than representing 'the nation,' which is supposed to supersede class and ethnic loyalties, these new governments represent coalitions of social classes and ethnic groups, especially—in Latin America—indigenous ethnic groups.[17]

The popular movements in Latin America are working to strengthen grass roots and traditional communitarian organizations. If this works, these organizations will be a balance to government and maybe—ultimately—a replacement for government.

I realize, as I write this, that it sounds like Marx and Engels: a proletarian government that functions as a transition to a genuinely communitarian/communist society. Well, it's always possible that Marx and Engels were right about this.

There is always the danger that revolutionaries put into power will become *apparatchiks*, as happened in the USSR and China. It is also possible that forces hostile to these new governments—the U.S. in Latin America, India and the U.S. in the case of Nepal—will be able to stop the popular movements.

Capitalism has been written off time and time again over the past two centuries. It is still with us, having—apparently—more lives than a cat. I am not willing to say it's finished. On the other hand, I hate the great lie formulated by Margaret Thatcher: TINA. There is no alternative.

Maybe capitalism will bumble along and continue to survive, possibly in the form of national police states or maybe, though this is unlikely, as a single world police state. Limited resources and social unrest are likely to require strong central administrations and centralized 'war' economies. The wars fought are likely to be against the poor.

Other alternatives exist, in spite of Margaret Thatcher. One is complete environmental and social collapse, which people like the NASA climate scientist James Hansen believe is possible and maybe even likely. Hansen is not a cheerful man these days. Another alternative is a genuinely popular and democratic society, in which capitalism and greed are defanged, and the world's resources are used to save humanity and the planet.

I suspect Wallerstein is right, and we are in a period of instability, in which real change in possible. So, what do we want? And—more to the point—which side are we on?

I am going to end with a quote by China Miéville, from the *Nebula Awards Showcase 2005*. He is talking about his particular sub-genre of speculative fiction, called New Weird:

> It's my opinion that the surge in the un-escapist, engaged fantastic, with its sense of limitless potentiality and the delighted bursting of boundaries, is an expression of a similar opening up of potentiality

in 'real life,' in politics. Neoliberalism collapsed the social imagination, stunting the horizons of the possible. With the crisis of the Washington Consensus and the rude grassroots democracies of the movements for social justice, millions of people are remembering what it is to imagine. That's why New Weird is post-Seattle fiction.[18]

I think of New Weird as fantasy, rather than classic science fiction. It may be easier to write fantasy these days, since real world change is so rapid and dramatic. How does one write about change when everything is changing?

But I think science fiction is still worth writing. It has its traditional roles: satire and cautionary tales, the exploration of the consequences of changing science and technology. But I think it would be a good idea if science fiction set the same goal as New Weird: breaking through boundaries and opening the horizons of the possible.

As Che said, "Let's be realists. Let's dream the impossible."

NOTES

1. My understanding of Immanuel Wallerstein comes from *The Decline of American Power, The U.S. in a Chaotic World* (New York: The New Press, 2003).

2. The founding parties in China and the USSR called themselves Communist Parties, but what they achieved was not communism. Nor did they claim it was, if I am remembering correctly. Communism was always in the future. What the USSR claimed to be was a socialist state. What was it in reality? 'Stalinist' and 'state capitalist' work as names. I am less sure about the exact nature of Mao's China, though the current economy looks like state capitalism.

3. I am not the only person to use this metaphor. Here is Paul Baran, quoted in *The Theory of Monopoly Capital* by John Bellamy Foster: "The trouble with economics is not that it does not yet 'know enough,' as its practitioners love to repeat. Its fatal shortcoming is that it does not incorporate in its knowledge the understanding of what is necessary for the attainment of a better, more rational economic order. Hemingway's Old Man was a virtuoso fisherman. If he had a fault, it was his incapacity to realize the overwhelming destructive power of the sharks."

4. When I wrote this originally I did not discuss the ways the Bush Administration increased government power: the Patriot Act, Homeland Security, the emphasis on the president as Commander in Chief with unlimited powers during an unending war... However, none of this legitimates a state. Instead, it turns the state into an incompetent tyranny, symbolized by Katrina and taking off one's shoes in airports.

5. William S. Lind, "Understanding Fourth Generation War," January 15, 2005, http://www.antiwar.com.

6. "First Declaration *of La Realidad* for Humanism and Against Neoliberalism," http://www.elzn.org.

7. The 2005 WTO meeting in Hong Kong was quieter and more satisfactory to the 'advanced' nations, which managed to get concessions from third world governments. However the Doha Round meeting in 2006, supposedly devoted to the interests of developing nations, ended in collapse due to the resistance of third world governments. Demonstrations continue to take place in response to world leadership meetings—during the Bali Climate Change Summit in 2007 (the English paper *The Independent* called these worldwide) and at the London and Pittsburgh G20 Conferences in 2009. More demonstrations are planned for the Copenhagen Climate Change Summit in December, 2009.

8. "Get Ready for $50 US Oil!!" *Energy Bulletin*, June 15, 2004 and "Shell Cuts Oil and Gas Reserves for the Fifth Time," *Energy Bulletin*, February 5, 2005.

9. *The Guardian*, November 9, 2009.

10. Stupidity is a possible alternative reason. As Hanlon's Razor tells us, "Never attribute to malice that which can be adequately explained by stupidity." Other reasons might be the need for a popular war to gain support for the Bush Administration and the need to justify expansion of the state's police powers. But I suspect these wars are resource wars.

11. A lot of this has to do with class—who has the world's money and control of the world's resources. This is a topic which deserves its own essay or its own book. I refer you to *Stagnation and the Financial Explosion* by Harry Magdoff and Paul M. Sweezy and *The Communist Manifesto* by Karl Marx and Frederick Engels.

12. The government's share of oil and gas revenue dropped from 50% to 18% after privatization.

13. The silver mine at Potosi in Bolivia produced 137 million pounds of silver between 1545 and 1835. This amazing wealth funded much of the economic development of Europe. The silver was mined by Indian and African slaves. It's estimated that the average miner lasted six months before he died, and that eight million workers died in Potosi. Though largely depleted, the mine is still worked today. Contemporary miners usually begin working in their teens, though there are younger children in the mine. Their life expectancy is 40.

14. James D. Cockcroft, "Indigenous Peoples Rising in Bolivia and Ecuador," *MRZine*. According to Wikipedia, only one Ecuadorian president was removed from power in this period. You pays your money, and you takes your choice. My inclination is to go with *MRZine*.

15. In addition to the struggles mentioned above, there are popular movements in rural India is response to the appropriation of land and water for industrial and commercial projects, such as hydroelectric dams and Coca Cola Company bottled water. And there are comparable actions in rural China, also in response to land loss. According to data

published by the Chinese government, there were 80,000 "protests, riots and mass actions" in 2008.

16. "Unionists Closely Watch Morales," *MRZine*, May 2, 2009. I have a favorite story about the 2005 election that brought Morales to power. A reporter talked with two Bolivian miners who had sticks of dynamite taped to their hard hats. The miners said, "If Morales doesn't do what we want, we'll throw him out and get someone who *will* do what we want." It's the dynamite that makes the story impressive. I would not want to mess with guys who wear exploding hats. I think the story comes from *National Geographic*, but I haven't been able to track down the specific article.

17. "Both nations' new constitutions distinguish between the old representative democracy and a new participatory and communitarian one. They call for plural nationhood; genuine interculturalism (instead of cosmetic multiculturalism); recognition of differences among cultures; and 'unity in diversity.' As a result, the native peoples' communities have constitutional rights to local self-governance and their own juridical procedures based on indigenous customs and traditions." James D. Cockcroft, "Indigenous Peoples Rising in Bolivia and Ecuador," *MRZine*.

18. *Nebula Awards Showcase 2005* (New York: Roc, 2005), 50.

"AT THE EDGE OF THE FUTURE"
ELEANOR ARNASON INTERVIEWED BY TERRY BISSON

What in your own background prepared you for being a writer of speculative fiction? Did living in an experimental dream house help?

I did grow up in an experimental house, built in 1947 to be a house of the future—the utopia that was going to happen, now that the Depression and the War were over. We had a garbage disposal, electric heat and central air, when these were futuristic. The furniture was cutting-edge modern, designed by Charles and Ray Eames, Isamu Noguchi, Alvar Aalto and so on.

It had been built by the Walker Art Center. When my father became director of the Walker in 1949, we moved into the house, which was right behind the museum. So I grew up in a design project house next to a contemporary art museum; and I grew up around artists. My father loved contemporary art, architecture and design; and he genuinely liked artists, which is not always true of art historians. He knew a lot of them, as well as designers like Charles and Ray Eames, and at least one engineer, Buckminster Fuller.

I came home from school one day and found Fuller holding court in the living room, surrounded by young college students. The Walker was building a geodesic dome at the time.

Kids always figure their life is the way life is. It never occurred to me that there was anything unusual or wonderful about finding Bucky Fuller in the living room.

So I grew up around people who were avant-gardists, which means—I guess—they lived at the edge of the future.

That was one reason I became an SF writer. Another was my mother, who was a feminist and a socialist. Like avant-gardists, socialists believe in the future.

Her parents were missionaries, and my mother grew up in a missionary community in western China. I don't think her parents were typical missionaries, since they seem to have been motivated by a belief in social justice and a genuine liking for the Chinese people. I got the impression from my mother that many of their fellow missionaries were bigots and lunatics. In any case, my mother always thought of China as her real home. She never had a bad word to say about the Chinese revolution. As far as she was concerned, anything that alleviated the terrible, evil poverty she saw as a child was okay.

(Chou En-lai was once asked his opinion of the French Revolution. He said he was waiting to see how it turned out. That is my opinion of the Chinese Revolution. But I never saw the poverty my mother did.)

My father's parents were from Iceland, which was primitive and desperately poor in the 19th and early 20th century. He grew up in an immigrant community in Canada, and somehow became an art historian fascinated by avant-garde culture.

What does this have to do with writing SF? Well both my parents moved from insular, pre-modern communities—the Icelandic immigrant community in Winnipeg, the missionary community in far western China—into modern America. For some reason they felt at home in the most progressive and avant-garde parts of American society. I think you could say they were travelers in time as well as space.

So I was raised by time travelers in a house of the future.

Finally, I fell in love with science fiction the first time I encountered it in the TV show *Captain Video* when I was eight or nine. I grew up reading SF. I think I liked it partly because it told me there was more to life than the claustrophobic, white bread society of the Minnesota; and partly because it was so realistic. I was living through the McCarthy period and through the period when there were fallout shelters and nuclear war drills in schools. Young children expected to die in a nuclear holocaust. That was their reality; and popular culture was stuff like *Father Knows Best* and *I Love Lucy*. SF talked about radioactive wastelands, and it talked about an American police state. It seemed true to life.

At what point did you decide to become a writer? How long was it between that and your first (or next) success?

I told stories to my kid brother before I was able to write. They were my stories, made up by me. After I learned to write, I wrote my stories down. That continued through high school and college. There was a period in my twenties when I mostly wrote poetry. Then in my late twenties I went back to fiction. I made my first short story sale to *New Worlds*, the legendary

English New Wave science fiction magazine edited by Michael Moorcock. In its last or almost-last incarnation *New Worlds* was an original anthology, edited by Charles Platt and published in the U.S. by Avon Books. I sold to this *New Worlds*, which was still a good publication.

I tend to think winning the Tiptree Award in 1992 was my first success. But this is not entirely true. My second published story, "The Warlord of Saturn's Moons," was a Nebula finalist; and the critic John Clute said kind things about my first novel. Maybe it would be more true to say I *felt* obscure until the Tiptree Award. It made a big difference to me.

How come an award for "feminist" SF is named after a guy?

Well, the Tiptree Award is named in honor of Alice Sheldon, who used the pen name of James Tiptree Jr. Sheldon did more than use a pen name. She posed as a man in her correspondence with many SF writers, editors and fans. She was finally outed by one of her correspondents, who was able to use the information in her letters to figure out her real life identity. Tiptree was never as comfortable in the SF community after she stopped being a man; and many people think her writing—which had been fabulous—declined in quality.

The award is for gender-bending speculative fiction. Tiptree seemed like the perfect person to honor. It's also a bit of a joke: the first SF award named after a woman is named after a woman who used a man's name.

Were you politically active in the '60s? In what way?

Yes, though I hung out with people who were far more serious than I was. I was in the Student Peace

Union during the "Ban the Bomb" period, before Vietnam became a serious issue. I remember riding down to Washington for a demonstration during the Cuban Missile Crisis, when we all thought we were going to die in a nuclear war. We were having a really depressing conversation. Someone finally said, "We have to stop talking about this. Has anyone seen a good movie lately?"

I said, "*Hiroshima Mon Amour.*"

I went on the 1963 Civil Rights March with my mother, a college friend and the college friend's mother. I didn't hear the famous "I have a dream" speech, because I convinced my mother to go to the National Gallery. I always finished demonstrations in Washington with a trip to a museum, or tried to.

My college was outside Philly, a short ride by commuter train, and I hung out with political activists in Philly. For the most part, they were members of the Young Peoples Socialist League, the youth group of the Socialist Party. They left the YPSL in the mid-'60s to form the American Socialist Organizing Committee, which had a brief life. After I moved to Detroit in 1968, I hung out with followers of C. L. R. James, a remarkable man and a wonderful writer. His best-known book is *The Black Jacobins*, a history of the slave revolution in Haiti that took place at the same time as the French Revolution.

My favorite book by him is *Mariners, Renegades, and Castaways: The Story of Herman Melville and the World We Live In*. James wrote most of it while being deported from the U.S. as an undesirable. I read *Moby Dick* as a result of James. His vision of the Pequod as an ocean-going factory, full of workers from all over the world, was compelling.

I knew members of the New Left, but they weren't my people. My friends—who were mostly in their twenties—came out of Old Left traditions and were still—in the 1960s—condemning Lenin and Trotsky for the way the new Soviet government treated sailors at the Kronstadt naval base in 1921. In 1917, the Kronstadt sailors had been heroes of the Revolution. In 1921, sailors at the base made what look to me like perfectly reasonable demands for a more democratic society (and one less dominated by the Bolshevik Party). Lenin and Trotsky sent in the Red Army to crush them.

I can understand that L and T were in serious trouble after the failure of revolution in the west. The isolated revolution in Russia, threatened by foreign armies and civil war, must have felt very precarious. But they shouldn't have been crushing revolutionary sailors. Power to the people!

I worked on a campaign for a third party candidate—an African American whose name I no longer remember—who was running for city council in New York. That was in 1963. A lot of the work was gathering signatures to get the candidate on the ballot. Because I was shy and reluctant to ask strangers for a signature, I was given the job of office manager at the campaign headquarters on the 125th Street in Harlem. I have a vivid memory of the night I couldn't get the door to lock. There I was on 125th Street. It was pitch black, and I couldn't leave the office unlocked. A couple of kind passersby got the door locked for me.

I was part of a group of college kids who gathered supplies for striking coal miners and ran the supplies down to eastern Kentucky. As with Harlem, what I mostly remember is how difficult it was for me to communicate with people I admired. The hills are their own world.

Mostly I read books and listened to people argue political theory. I was more comfortable with words and ideas.

The '60s were long ago. Have you been politically active since then?

On and off. Mostly, I have been active where I lived and worked—I was a shop steward in an art museum and a hat factory, a local and national official in the National Writers Union, in DFL precinct politics when Patrick and I owned a house.

I should mention that the DFL is the Democratic Farmer Labor Party, the Minnesota version of the Democratic Party. It was formed by a merger of the Farmer Labor Party and the Democratic Party in 1944.

This is a quote from Floyd B. Olson, Farmer Labor governor of Minnesota, speaking on the steps of the state capitol in 1933:

> I am making a last appeal to the Legislature. If the Senate does not make provision for the sufferers in the State and the Federal Government refuses to aid, I shall invoke the powers I hold and shall declare martial law. . . . A lot of people who are now fighting [relief] measures because they happen to possess considerable wealth will be brought in by provost guard and be obliged to give up more than they would now. There is not going to be misery in this State if I can humanly prevent it. . . Unless the Federal and State governments act to insure against recurrence of the present situation, I hope the present system of government goes right down to hell.

And this is from Wikipedia:

> During his three terms as governor, Olson pro-
> posed, and the legislature passed, bills that insti-
> tuted a progressive income tax, created a social se-
> curity program for the elderly, expanded the state's
> environmental conservation programs, guaranteed
> equal pay for women and the right to collective
> bargaining, and instituted a minimum wage and a
> system of unemployment insurance.

Mostly, the DFL is another Democratic Party.
But there something left from the Farmer Labor party,
how much I am never sure. The progressive wing of the
DFL remembers the party's Farmer Labor roots.

*Did your artistic side propel you into politics, or was it the
other way around?*

Given my background, the two went hand-in-
hand.

Like Hansel and Gretel?

Yes, though I don't remember leaving a trail of
breadcrumbs. I don't like leaving tracks.

*How would you describe your education? What were your
most productive (not favorite) fields of study?*

My formal education was the University of
Minnesota's experimental grade school and high
school, plus Swarthmore College and grad school at the
University of Minnesota. My undergrad and grad major
was art history. I like art history, because it positions art

in a historical context. Art doesn't float above the real world like a Platonic form. It is rooted in a specific age and society and social class.

But my real education came from my parents, the activists I knew in the '60s, and the people I worked with in office jobs in Detroit.

I started writing seriously in Detroit. After I moved back to Minneapolis, I continued to work office jobs, along with some rather nice warehouse jobs; and I kept writing, though always slowly.

I gradually acquired a skill—full charge bookkeeping—and got better jobs, which took more time and energy. For a period of about ten years I wrote very little. I'm trying to get back to writing, now that I am unemployed.

And with undiminished artistry it seems. Mammoths *is a story within a story, told by one character to another. Is that structure a departure for you?*

I like embedded stories. But I have never done anything exactly like *Mammoths*, where the whole story is being told with quote marks, so the reader never forgets the frame setting in Fort Yates on the Standing Rock Reservation.

A lot of real history is told to us, how our parents grew up, what they did during the war. And Native Americans really respect oral tradition. I didn't plan this—in fact, I just thought of it—but I am describing a classic form of Native American learning, a kid listening to an elder, who is likely to be an elder relative.

In Ring of Swords *and* A Woman of the Iron People *we see alien cultures through the eyes of scientists or diplomats from Earth. I find the society they left behind as mysteri-*

ous and wonderful as the one they are investigating. You suggest utopian elements that remind me of Marge Piercy's Woman on the Edge of Time. *What a peculiar, and wonderful, way to construct a utopia, almost as if it is seen in peripheral vision. Can you talk a little about the Earth your far travelers leave behind?*

I'm not sure about the Earth in *A Woman of the Iron People*. My travelers have been on a starship for two hundred years, and Earth has changed a lot during this period. I suspect society there has moved past socialism to something post-socialist, maybe a communist utopia, though the people on the ship think the new society back home is more than a little nuts.

I'm working on a sequel to *Ring of Swords*, which begins on Earth, and it is making me crazy, because I have to describe the society on Earth, and I am stuck with what I wrote in *Ring of Swords*. Earth has nine billion people, and it is still a class society. But it hasn't fallen apart, which I suspect it would have. Instead, people are trucking along, doing the best they can, dealing with the environmental mess we left them. My current theory is, the rich have moved to space colonies where they live surrounded by their middle class servants: doctors, lawyers, artists, scientists and hair stylists.

(They don't have all the professionals, but they have the ones who are into serious luxury. Earth is a place of rules and limitations. It has to be, in order to keep nine billion people fed and housed and living okay lives.)

The rich are left alone, because it's too much trouble to destroy the space colonies. I assume they have some power, but I don't know how much. I think the Earth in this novel is something like a Scandinavian social democracy, though maybe with less money.

The novel is set about 150 years in the future. The decisions we make now will determine that future, which means my idea of the future keeps shifting as I watch contemporary politics. If global warming continues along its current route, Africa is going to be arid and deeply impoverished. An official from Senegal at the Copenhagen Climate Summit said the behavior of the rich countries—refusing to deal with global warming and letting the nations of Africa face death by starvation and war—was like the Holocaust. The rich countries were outraged, of course. How dare this person compare what's happening to Africa to the Holocaust? The Holocaust was a real tragedy and crime.

Anyway, one of the important characters in the novel is from Harare. So I need to think about her Africa.

Can you explain why you favored this indirect approach to world-building?

Maybe because I'm habitually oblique. I can write a straightforward story, I suppose. But in most of my writing, I use indirection to find direction out.

As mentioned above, it's hard to figure what our future will be and how we will get there. It's easier to do an end run around the problem.

In Woman of the Iron People *you describe a world with no cities and no wars. Is that a utopia? Most of your books have happy endings. Is that a political position or an artistic propensity, or both?*

No wars would be great. It certainly looks utopian from here. I like cities, but I think they need to be smaller or at least much more compact than contemporary American cities. Right now, we need to preserve every bit of arable land we have, so we can use it for farming. This probably means very dense urban areas. But we are also going to have to stop relying on long-distance shipping. So maybe we will have small, dense cities that can live off the surrounding land. Or bigger cities with lots of gardens.

I am in favor of happy endings in fiction and real life. I think people need to believe that life can be better than it is right now.

Do you have a regimen or routine for writing? Do you like doing first drafts or revisions most? (Or dislike one of these least?)

I am trying to create a routine, in order to up production. Right now, I tend to write when I feel like it, which is not often enough.

In general, I like writing the first draft, because that's when I find out what the story is about.

I used to do three drafts, the first handwritten, the second typed with handwritten revisions all over it, and the third a clean typewritten manuscript which I could send out.

Now, I mostly work on a computer and revise as I write, so there are no longer three distinct drafts. I write a few pages, print them out, revise by hand, input the revisions and continue. If I don't do this, I begin each session at the computer by revising the last section I wrote, then continuing. It's back and forth, like sewing with a lock stitch.

After I have a complete story, I run it though my workshop. They suggest changes. I input most of their changes and maybe a few of my own. Then the almost-final version of the story goes to my agent, who may suggest a few more changes.

Your novels are unusual in that the characters take time out to pee. Would your mother approve?

My family loved food and eating. What goes in must come out in some form sooner or later. I think my mother was realistic enough to know that. And I got my love of American plumbing from somewhere. I wouldn't be surprised if it came from my mother, who grew up without it.

There was talk of a sequel to Ring of Swords. *Where is that now? Does it have a title?*

Hearth World.
It's set on Earth and on the alien home world—two hearths for two different species.
I'm revising it, and going crazy trying to figure out the Earth society. Also, the novel is too dark right now. I have to make it happier.

What writers were most influential in getting you under-way? Who are the most influential today?

The writers I remember from my childhood are William Tenn, Philip K. Dick, Cyril Kornbluth, Frederik Pohl, Avram Davidson, Fritz Leiber, Robert Sheckley, Leigh Brackett... The New Wave writers were important later, then the women writers of the 1970s. I read Samuel R. Delany and very much admired his work, also the people published in *New Worlds*. I especially liked

John Sladek, who was from my part of the country, though he lived in England for years. John was a brilliant and brilliantly funny writer who died too young. I read Suzy McKee Charnas and Joanna Russ, Octavia Butler, James Tiptree Jr. and all the women writers who began publishing in the 1960s and '70s. Ursula K. Le Guin has been the most important influence. When people ask me what my writing is like, I say it's like Le Guin.

As the first winner of the Tiptree Award, you have been deeply involved in the feminist movement in SF. Can you give us an idea of that and how it developed?

I wasn't active in the feminist movement in fandom in the really hot period, during the late '60s and early '70s. I was out of touch with the science fiction community at the time. However, my fiction is feminist, and I have done a lot of panels at cons, starting in the mid '70s when I moved back to Minneapolis and reconnected with science fiction fandom. A lot of panels have been about women's issues, gay and lesbian issues, race and racism in science fiction, class issues in science fiction.

I guess you could a lot of my political activity since the late 1970s has been talking politics in the science fiction community.

When I went to my first science fiction convention in 1961, fandom was entirely white and 80 percent male. Women were marginalized as "femfans." Gay people were in the closet. The history of the community since then has been the painful assimilation of women, GLBT people, people of color…

If science fiction is going to be a real community—and a real literature that matters to the real world—it has to deal with prejudice and class.

There is an anthropological bent to most of your SF. Is that from your own original inclinations, or does it reflect the influence of Le Guin? Or both?

I've certainly been influenced by Le Guin, also by Marx and Engels in *The German Ideology*, where they argue that

> People are the producers of their conceptions and ideas—real, active people, as they are conditioned by the development of their productive forces and of the intercourse corresponding to these, out to its farthest forms. Consciousness can never be anything else except conscious existence; and the existence of people is what they actually, physically do in the concrete universe. Life is not determined by consciousness, but consciousness by life.

In other words, I am interested in the relationship between ideology, technology and the organization of everyday life.

I'm also interested in alienation and disjuncture— the people who don't fit in, the moments in history when tradition is not adequate to deal with new realities.

I think all of this is anthropology, though it isn't the study of unchanging, traditional societies; rather it is the study of societies on the move.

A critic once described you as a poet of "the beautiful and the loony." Was this a friendly comment?

Yes.

There is a lot of humor in your work, but it's unannounced (i.e., dry). There's no laugh track, or as you say in "Mam-

moths," you are not going to point out the jokes.. Is this because you are sneaky, or just classy?

I didn't realize I was telegraphing my humor technique in *Mammoths*. But yes, you are right, that line tells the reader exactly what I do.

Part of this is my habitual sneakiness. The other part is Scandinavian and Scandinavian-American humor, which is often deadpan.

Tell me something about the Rivendell group. How come Minneapolis has such an active SF/Fantasy community? Is it the weather?

If it's the weather, we are in trouble, because the weather is getting warmer.

Rivendell happened and continues to happen because of David Lenander. He has done most of the work. David also maintains websites for several local authors and critics, including one for me. I am very grateful to him for this.

The local science fiction semi-prozine *Tales of the Unanticipated* is due to Eric Heideman, though Eric has had help over the years. TOTU's poetry editors—Terry Garey and Rebecca Korvo—have been excellent. Eric is also responsible for a lot of the serious literary programming at local science fiction cons.

Ruth Berman and I started the oldest local SF fiction-writing group in the 1970s; and it was really hard to get it going. There were far fewer writers and aspiring writers in the Twin Cities then.

Other writing groups appeared later. I am in two at the moment, one for poetry and one for fiction.

Then there are all the people who worked on

Minicon, back when Eric and I were active on the con committee, and who split off to form new conventions.

Once you have an environment where writing is taken seriously, more writers begin to appear. Fandom is always full of people who love science fiction and dream of writing it.

Isn't Rivendell more fantasy than SF? Or do you make those distinctions? How does the Mythopoeic Society fit in? Do you feel at home in SF today?

I read and write both fantasy and science fiction. There are obvious differences between the two, but the writers I grew up with wrote both. American fantasy has two roots, I think: Tolkien and science fiction. Like science fiction, it builds worlds that are more or less logical, given the premises. I suppose you could call it pedestrian, one-foot-after-another fantasy, as opposed to the wild flights of surrealism and magic realism. When it doesn't work, American fantasy plods. When it does work, it has many of the pleasures of science fiction.

David Lenander, the guy responsible for Rivendell, is an old friend of mine; and other old friends belong. So I feel very much at home there.

I feel at home with the people at the Wiscon science fiction convention, which bills itself as the only feminist SF convention in the world, and with much of the Twin Cities science fiction community, especially the people who split off from Minicon during the Big Blowup. I was involved in an extended struggle within the Minicon con comm in the 1980s. The struggle was between people who wanted to open the con up and create a more diverse local fandom, and the people who wanted to keep local fandom the way it was: white, straight, male dominated and hostile to media fans.

The people who split off formed three new conventions, all of which welcome diversity, and all of which are rolling along quite nicely. Minicon has shrunk from three thousand attendees to about four hundred. It has survived thus far, though it's been a struggle. I told them years ago they weren't going to last if they relied on aging, straight, white fans. Mortality gets you every time.

I have mixed feelings about the SF community outside the Upper Midwest. Sometimes I feel close to it, and sometimes it ticks me off.

How come?

Boy, a hard question. Partly, I often feel out-of-place in the larger science fiction community. I don't like going out to dinner with forty other people. I'd sooner have breakfast with a couple of people, especially at Wiscon.

I like the SF community when it is open-minded and open to the world—liberal in the oldest sense, with the same root as liberation and liberty. I like it when it deals with serious questions, such as the nature of our current society and our future, if any. It can do this through humor and satire. Many of the best SF writers are very funny.

I don't like the science fiction community when it's narrow and closed-in and trivial.

How come so many of your characters are furry or hairy (including the mammoths of the Great Plains)? Is it because St. Paul is so cold?

I am trying to use more scales and feathers, because readers confuse my various furry aliens. I grew up with cats, and I love the furry little critters. I think my love of fur comes from them.

There's more than one way to skin a cat.

I would never even think of skinning a cat. It sounds horrible. But I have more mittens than I need already.

Your first book had a dragon in it, I believe. Does that mean you started as a fantasy author? It was a small one.

As I remember, there is no magic in *The Sword Smith*. The dragons are intelligent therapod dinosaurs, and the trolls are hominids of some kind, maybe Neanderthals. So that book was science fiction disguised as fantasy. My third novel—*Daughter of the Bear King*—was fantasy, but the editor labeled it as science fiction on the spine, because "it felt like science fiction" to him.

I write both quite happily, and like stories that mix science fiction with fantasy.

Do you do hack work or media work in addition to SF? Have you done comics, kids books, other peripheral SF genre stuff?

No. I might enjoy doing some of this, but I write too slowly.

Any movie options? A Woman of the Iron People *would make a great road movie.*

Nope. Nothing of mine has ever been optioned. I understand the money for the option is great, but actually getting a movie made can be painful.

There are references in your work to poets such as John Donne and Gerard Manley Hopkins. What poets do you read for fun? Do you write poetry? Do you do readings?

Right now I am reading Bill Holm, the wonderful Icelandic American poet who just died. I'm also reading Freya Manfred, another Minnesota poet, and Louis Jenkins, yet another Minnesota poet. I very much like the North Dakotan Thomas McGrath, who was a great 20th century American poet, I think, who has been undervalued because of his politics. Tom was an unreconstructed Stalinist. He once almost ripped my head off, because I said something nice about Trotsky. But he loved "no war but the class war," which is a line Trotsky wrote. I didn't tell him this.

I do write poetry, and I belong to a poetry workshop, which does performances at cons under the name "Lady Poetesses from Hell." (The group includes two men, but women are the majority.) We are working—very slowly—on an anthology. The people in the group are *good* poets.

You refer in Woman of the Iron People *to the Finland Station. Is this in Moscow, Leningrad or Outer Space?*

In the novel it's a space station. Obviously, it's a joke—and a reference to the train station in Petrograd where Lenin arrived at the start of the Bolshevik Revolution. He had been in exile in Switzerland. Trotsky was in Brooklyn when the revolution began, a fact I love.

In an interview you once expressed annoyance with far future novels that are based on today's science, and your works are often set in the near (or an alternate near) future. Does that make you part of the "Mundane" movement in SF?

I don't think so. My irritation is with the hard science fiction writers, who take so much pride in having their science right, even though it's 20th century science and their story is set thousands of years in the future. Most of these writers are guys, and their societies are often quite traditional. The characters have Anglo-Saxon names, like the characters in 1940s pulp science fiction stories. The society they live in is like our society now or like American society in the 1950s. This is ridiculous.

All human societies change. You can see this in changing stone tools during the Paleolithic. You can see it in art and architecture from the Neolithic on. How do you think art historians date most art? By the technology and techniques used and by the style, all of which change.

I have nothing against far future SF and off-the-wall, almost-magical SF. Just realize that technology changes society, and weird technologies are going to create weird societies.

Also realize that real science in the far future is going to involve ideas and machines we can't imagine, any more than 16th-century scientists could imagine Relativity and the Large Hadron Collider.

I haven't liked the term "Mundane Science Fiction" since Geoff Ryman almost made me crazy a few years back by saying that nanotechnology is impossible and not worth writing about. All nanotechnology means is "very small technology," and it's happening right now. Scientists are designing machines made from molecules and atoms, and they are doing things with viruses and genes that are changing the world.

Most of us may remain human, because gene mod might well be expensive. But I don't think the rich are going to be human in the future; and if they need modified servants, they will get them.

I tend to stick to the next couple of hundred years, because I don't want to twist my brain into knots trying to figure out where science and society are going to be in the far future.

If you could read in any language other than English, what would it be?

I already read French, though not so well, and Icelandic with a dictionary in hand. I'd like to be able to read Icelandic fluently, so I could read the sagas in the original, also modern Icelandic poetry. I'd like to read Chinese poetry in the original, but I understand classical Chinese poetry is insanely difficult, even if you are fluent in the language.

Why?

Chinese because China was my mother's home, and I love Chinese poetry in translation, and because it's a really different language.

Icelandic because it was the language of my father's ancestors, and I love the Icelandic sagas. I took medieval Icelandic in graduate school. It's a Germanic language, as is English, which makes it a lot easier than many languages. One of my plans for retirement is to settle down with a dictionary and the *Grettis Saga Asmundarsonar* in normalized Old Norse and keep translating till I can read Icelandic easily. Of course, the Icelandic I will be able to read is 13th century Icelandic. I will then have to learn the 20th century vocabulary.

Have you traveled a lot as an SF author? Where to. Have you ever been to Iceland?

No. I traveled a lot as a kid with my parents. Now I stick to trips around the Upper Midwest and visits to New England and the Bay Area, where I have relatives. I've been to Iceland twice. I'm interested in Latin America—Costa Rica for the birding, Venezuela and Bolivia for the politics, Cuba because it's supposed to have a sustainable economy, the only one in the world. I hear Cuban music is awesome.

A lot of your work has to do with aliens and alienated people, in other cultures than their own. Yet you live in the same city where you were born and raised. Explain.

I was born in New York. As a kid, I lived in New York, Chicago, Washington, D.C., London, Paris, Chicago again, St. Paul, Minneapolis, Paris again, Minneapolis again, Honolulu, and Minneapolis again. Some of these stays were only a few months. Others were years.

I spent six weeks in Kabul as a kid, which is not long enough to say I lived in Afghanistan. But it shows up in my writing. A beautiful, utterly amazing country.

As an adult, I went to college in the Philly area, then moved back to Minneapolis, then to New York, then to Detroit, then back to Minneapolis. I now live in St. Paul.

So, I did a fair amount of traveling before I was thirty-three and very little since then, except around the

Upper Midwest. There's a lot in the Upper Midwest. I figure you can know only a few places well.

But I should travel more. That's on the to-do list.

The plus side of my upbringing is—I learned to dislike prejudice and believe in justice, to love art and take joy in the range of human cultures, above all the range of human food. My family ate its way around the world in 1959 and enjoyed every bite. The downside is, I didn't fit into the very white, midwestern culture of Minnesota in the 1950s.

That sense of not belonging is still with me. I have never thought that I understood Americans as a group. (I am not entirely sure they are a group. Minnesota has more in common with Manitoba than it does with the southern half of the U.S.) But I am in many ways a product of Minnesota and of this part of North America. I guess you could say I am both rooted and alienated.

Rosa in *Mammoths* is like this.

Why am I still in the Twin Cities? They are more affordable than New York and safer than Detroit. The weather's better than Seattle. The greater metro area sprawls way too much, but the two core cities are reasonably sized. There are three good art museums, two good orchestras, a perfectly adequate opera company, two good city park systems, and a lot of good regional parks. There are many theaters and lakes. Bald eagles nest along the Mississippi in the metro area. I see wild turkeys now and then, along with lots of hawks and herons. I understand Minnesotans as well as I understand anyone; and my friends are here.

Do you read mostly fiction or nonfiction? What sort of fiction do you read?

It's fifty-fifty. I read science fiction, fantasy and detective novels. Very little "literary" fiction, unless it is fantastic. My nonfiction is science and politics. I love books about biology, evolution and dinosaurs.

Do you have any hobbies? I hope not.

Bird watching. I became a bird watcher after I discovered birds are descended from dinosaurs and can be called living dinosaurs. The love of my youth was returned to me—smaller and able to fly. I am not a fanatic. I do not keep lists. But looking for birds makes me notice my environment more, and I do love having dinosaurs around.

What kind of car do you drive? There are not many guns or machines in your work. How come?

I don't drive, which is weird and hard to explain. The household car is a Saturn SL1 with 170,000 miles on it.

I don't like guns. When I lived in Detroit, lots of people were armed, and the murder rate was eight hundred a year. I didn't see that the guns made life better.

Fiction is a way for people to think about their lives and imagine ways to change their lives. Most of the violence in science fiction isn't helpful. It doesn't work as an example of how to change the world.

I am not sure that violence is always a mistake. But you had better be very careful how you use it. It can easily lead to really dire consequences.

If there is kind of violence I feel comfortable with, it's the kind used historically by working people: tossing a sabot into the gearing or a spanner in the works.

Obviously, working class violence can go beyond this. The father of one my friends in college was a CP thug in the 1930s. He and his buddies would beat up fascists in New York City. Was this wrong? I leave it to you to decide. Fascists are very dangerous. And I remember being told that you can't run an unarmed picket line in eastern Kentucky. Still and all, workers are more likely to rely on fists, bricks, bottles and sabotage. The bosses do most of the shooting and killing.

(I can think of outright labor wars: the famous war between mine bosses and the Western Federation of Miners in Colorado early in the 20th century. But I just checked Wikipedia, and it sounds as if most of the violence—especially the violence directed toward people—came from the bosses and the state government.)

I don't have a lot of machines in my fiction because I don't understand machinery well enough to imagine future machines. I do have a dragon flush toilet in my first novel, and there's a fair amount of plumbing in my fiction. The modern American bathroom is a wonder, though it wastes far too much water.

Do you go to a lot of movies?

No, though I like some anime, especially Miyazaki, and the Aardman movies, especially *Chicken Run*, which is the best socialist chicken movie I have ever seen. I love *WALL-E*.

Going to more movies is on my to-do list, along with going to more plays and museums and traveling more.

What do you think of Al Franken? Barack Obama? Sharon Olds?

I like Al Franken and have hope for him. He might turn out to be a good progressive. Though this might not be adequate. I am starting to think the country may well swing either far right or far left. If far right, Al may end up like his friend Paul Wellstone. If far left, he may turn out to be too much of a centrist.

My opinion of Barack Obama is not fit for a family publication.

Sharon Olds the poet? I don't know her work, though I will now look it up. She turned down an invitation to the White House. Everyone should. It's not a decent place to visit.

Do you believe in life after death? During? Before?

I believe in life during life. Death seems real and may be useful. I began to like mortality, when I realized it was the only way to get rid of the leaders of the American union movement. But I don't like personal mortality and would like to live long enough to see how this century turns out.

BIBLIOGRAPHY

NOVELS

The Sword Smith. New York: Condor Press, 1978.

To the Resurrection Station. New York: Avon Books, 1986.

Daughter of the Bear King. New York: Avon Books, 1987.

A Woman of the Iron People. New York: William Morrow, 1991.
        Tiptree Award winner. Winner of Mythopoeic Society Award for best adult fantasy. Third place, Campbell Award for best science fiction novel.

Ring of Swords. New York: Tor Books, 1993.
        Winner of Minnesota Book Award for best fantasy & science fiction. Tiptree Award short list.

Tomb of the Fathers: A Lydia Duluth Adventure. Seattle: Aqueduct Press, 2010.

CHAPBOOKS

The Grammarian's Five Daughters. Minneapolis: Minnesota Center for Book Arts, 2005.

Mammoths of the Great Plains. Oakland: PM Press, 2010.

COLLECTION

Ordinary People. Seattle: Aqueduct Press, 2005.

MISCELLANEOUS SHORT FICTION

"A Clear Day in the Motor City." In *New Worlds* 5. New York: Avon Books, 1973. Reprinted in *The New, Improved Sun.* New York: Harper & Row, 1975.

"The Warlord of Saturn's Moons." In *New Worlds* 6. New York: Avon Books, 1974. Reprinted in *The New Women of Wonder.* New York: Vintage Books, 1978. Reprinted in *The Norton Book of Science Fiction.* New York: W.W. Norton & Co., 1993. Reprinted in *Ordinary People.* Nebula Award finalist.

"Ace 167." In *Orbit* 15. New York: Harper & Row, 1974.

"The House by the Sea." In *Orbit* 16. New York: Harper & Row, 1974.

"The Face on the Barroom Floor." With Ruth Berman. In *Star Trek: The New Voyages*. New York: Bantam Books, 1976.

"Going Down." In *Orbit* 19. New York: Harper & Row, 1977.

"A Ceremony of Discontent." *A Room of One's Own* 6, no. 1 and 2 (1981). Reprinted in *The Women Who Walk Through Fire*. Freedom, Ca.: The Crossing Press, 1992. Reprinted in *Ordinary People*.

"The Ivory Comb." In *Amazons II*. New York: DAW Books, 1982. Reprinted in *Stiller's Pond*. Minneapolis: New Rivers Press, 1988.

"Glam's Story." *Tales of the Unanticipated* (Spring 1987).

"Among the Featherless Bipeds." *Tales of the Unanticipated* (Winter/Spring 1988).

"A Brief History of St. Cyprian the Athlete." *Tales of the Unanticipated.* (Spring/Summer/Fall 1992), http://www.tc.umn.edu/~d-lena/StCyprian.html.

"The Dog's Story." *Asimov's Science Fiction* (July 1996). Reprinted in *Isaac Asimov's Camelot*. New York: Ace Books, 1998. Reprinted in *The Mammoth Book of Arthurian Legends*. London: Robinson Publishing, 1998. Nebula Award finalist.

"The Venetian Method." *Tales of the Unanticipated* (August 1998–July 1999). Reprinted in *Best of the Rest*. Boston: Suddenly Press, 1999.

"The Grammarian's Five Daughters." *Realms of Fantasy* (June 1999). Reprinted in *The Year's Best Fantasy and Horror* 13. New York: St. Martin's Press, 2000. Reprinted in *Ordinary People*. Also published in *Strange Horizons*, March 29, 2004. World Fantasy Award finalist. http://www.strangehorizons.com/2004/20040329/grammarian.shtml.

"Big Black Mama and Tentacle Man." *Tales of the Unanticipated* (July 2003–July 2004). Reprinted in *New Wyrd*. Minneapolis/St. Paul: The Wyrdsmiths, 2006.

"Big Ugly Mama and the Zk." *Asimov's Science Fiction* (September 2003).

"Big Green Mama Falls in Love." In *Eidolon I*. North Perth: Eidolon Books, 2006.

"The Diner." *Tales of the Unanticipated* (Autumn/Winter 2008).

"Patrick and Mr. Bear." *Tales of the Unanticipated* (2010).

HWARHATH SHORT FICTION

"The Hound of Merin." In *Xanadu*. New York: Tor Books, 1993.

"The Lovers." *Asimov's Science Fiction* (July 1994). Reprinted in *Flying Cups and Saucers*. Cambridge, Mass: Edgewood Press, 1998. Reprinted in *Isaac Asimov's Val-*

entines. New York: Ace Books,1999. Reprinted in *Ordinary People*. Tiptree Award short list.

"The Semen Thief." *Amazing Stories* (Winter 1994).

"The Small Black Box of Morality." *Tales of the Unanticipated* (Spring/Summer/Fall 1996), http://www.tc.umn.edu/~d-lena/SmallBlackBox.html. Reprinted in *Women of Other Worlds*. Nedlands: University of Western Australia Press, 1999. Reprinted in *Ordinary People*.

"Introduction to Ten Examples of Contemporary Hwarhath Fiction." *Paradoxa* 4, no. 10 (1998).

"The Gauze Banner." In *More Amazing Stories*. New York: Tor Books, 1998. Tiptree Award short list.

"Dapple," *Asimov's Science Fiction* (September 1999). Reprinted in *The Year's Best Science Fiction* 17. New York: St. Martin's Press, 2000. Winner of Spectrum Award for best short fiction. Sturgeon Award finalist.

"The Actors." *Fantasy and Science Fiction* (December 1999). Tiptree Award long list.

"Origin Story." *Tales of the Unanticipated* (April 2000–April 2001). Reprinted in *Ordinary People.*

"The Potter of Bones." *Asimov's Science Fiction* (September 2002), http://www.asimovs.com/_issue_0401/bones.shtml. Reprinted in *The Year's Best Science Fiction* 20. New York: St. Martin's Press, 2003. Nebula Award finalist.

"The Garden." In *Synergy*. Waterville, ME: Five Star, 2004. Reprinted in *The Year's Best Science Fiction* 22. New York: St. Martin's Press, 2005. Reprinted in *Best Short Fiction 2005*. Garden City: Science Fiction Book Club, 2005.

STORIES IN THE LYDIA DULUTH UNIVERSE

"Stellar Harvest." *Asimov's Science Fiction* (April 1999). Reprinted in *Nebula Awards Showcase 2002*. New York: St. Martin's Griffin, 2002. Winner of HOMer Award. Hugo Award and Nebula Award finalist.

"The Cloud Man." *Asimov's Science Fiction* (October/ November 2000).

"Lifeline." *Asimov's Science Fiction* (February 2001).

"The Glutton, A Goxhat Accounting Chant." *Tales of the Unanticipated* (April 2001-April 2002).

"Moby Quilt." *Asimov's Science Fiction* (May 2001). Reprinted in *The Year's Best Science Fiction* 19. New York: St. Martin's Griffin, 2002.

"The Lost Mother." *Tales of the Unanticipated* (April 2002-April 2003).

"Knapsack Poems." *Asimov's Science Fiction* (May 2002), http://www.asimovs.com/_issue_0401/knapsack.shtml. Reprinted in *The Year's Best SF* 8. New York: Eos, 2003. Tiptree Award short list. Nebula Award finalist.

SELECTED POETRY

"OKAY FELLA THIS IS IT." In *Only Humans with Songs to Sing*. New York: Smyrna Press, 1969.

"Song of the Shipping Department." *The Mill Hunk Herald* (The Cold Months, 1983-1984). Reprinted in *Labor's Joke Book*. St. Louis: WD Press, 1985. Reprinted in *Overtime*. Albuquerque: West End Press, 1990.

"The Land of Ordinary People." In *Looking for Utopia*. New York: Schocken Books, 1985. Reprinted in *Ordinary People*.

"On the Border." In *Time Gum*. Minneapolis: Rune Press, 1988.

"Amnita and the Giant Stinginess." *Tales of the Unanticipated* (Spring/Summer/Fall 1990).

"Bus Poem." In *Everyday Poems for City Sidewalk*. St. Paul: St. Paul Public Works and Public Art St. Paul, 2008. Also printed in a concrete sidewalk block.

INTERVIEWS AND ESSAYS

"The Work Community." *Radical America* 5, no. 4 (1971). Published under nom de plume L. Valmeras.

"An Interview with Eleanor Arnason by Eric Heideman." *Tales of the Unanticipated* (Fall 1986).

"On Writing Science Fiction." In *Women of Vision*. New York: St. Martin's Press, 1988.

"In Defense of Science Fiction." In *A View from the Loft* (January 1993).

"On Writing *A Woman of the Iron People*." In *Monad* 3. Eugene, Ore: Pulphouse Publishing, 1993.

"Interview with Eleanor Arnason by Lyda Morehouse." In *Strange Horizon*, March 29, 2004.

"Writing Science Fiction during the Third World War." Guest of Honor Speech at Wiscon 28. Reprinted in *Ordinary People*. Seattle: Aqueduct Press, 2005. Also published in *The Infinite Matrix*, January 23, 2006. An earlier version of the speech appeared in *Extrapolation* 46, no. 1.

ESSAYS ABOUT THE WORK OF ELEANOR ARNASON

Attebery, Brian. "Ring of Swords: A Reappreciation." *The New York Review of Science Fiction*, April 2004, http://www.tc.umn.edu/~d-lena/Ring_of_Swords_Arnason.html.

Berman, Ruth. "Humor in Eleanor Arnason's Ring of Hwarhath Stories." *Strange Horizons*, March 29, 2004, http://www.strangehorizons.com/2004/20040329/hwarhath.shtml.

Gordon, Joan. "Incite/On-Site/Insight: Implications of the Other in Eleanor Arnason's Science Fiction." In *Future Females: The Next Generation*. Lanham: Rowman & Littlefield, 2000.

ABOUT THE AUTHOR

Eleanor Arnason was born in New York City in 1942. Her mother, Elizabeth Hickcox Yard, was a social worker who grew up in a missionary community in western China. Her father, Hjorvardur Harvard Arnason, was the son of Icelandic immigrants and an art historian.

She got her interest in art, literature, music, history and social justice from her parents. She isn't sure where her interest in science comes from. Maybe from the curiosity which her parents encouraged or maybe from science fiction, which she loved from the first moment she saw *Captain Video* on TV.

She spent her early childhood living in New York, Chicago, Washington, D.C., London, Paris and St. Paul. In 1949 her father became director of the Walker Art Center in Minneapolis; and her family moved into a house of the future which the Walker had built as a postwar design project. Ms. Arnason lived in the house (which was named Idea House # 2) until 1960.

She graduated from Swarthmore College with a B.A. in art history in 1964 and attended graduate school at the University of Minnesota until 1967, when she left the university to find out about life outside colleges and art museums.

From 1967 to 1974 she worked as an office clerk and lived in racially-mixed, blue-collar neighborhoods, first in central Brooklyn, then in Detroit. This was the era when the American cities were burning, when black auto workers in Detroit were organizing DRUM (the Dodge Revolutionary Union Movement) and when the Wayne State University student newspaper had as its masthead, "One class conscious worker is worth 10,000 students." Ms. Arnason learned a lot about the world outside art museums. She made her first professional sale, a short story, to *New Worlds,* in 1972.

In 1974 she decided Detroit was looking at hard times. The American car industry was under strong pressure from foreign auto manufacturers. It seemed clear to her that the Big Three were going to need new plants in order to remain competitive; and it was unlikely the plants would be built in Detroit. The city's inhabitants were too class conscious and feisty. She moved back to Minneapolis, bringing with her Patrick Arden Wood, a fine product of the Detroit working class who has remained her close friend and comrade.

Since 1974 she has remained in the Twin Cities, working in offices, warehouses, a large art museum and (in recent years) a series of small nonprofits devoted to history, peace and justice and art.

Her first novel, *The Sword Smith*, was published in 1978. Other novels followed: *To the Resurrection Station* in 1986, *Daughter of the Bear King* in 1987, *A Woman of the Iron People* in 1991, and *Ring of Swords* in 1993.

Since 1994, Ms. Arnason has concentrated on short fiction, creating two series of linked stories, one about an alien species called the hwarhath, and the other about an interstellar adventurer named Lydia Duluth. She is also working on a series of science fictional tall tales about the Big Mamas, large and powerful trickster spirits who are able to travel through time and space.

She belongs to two writing groups: the Wyrdsmiths (science fiction and fantasy prose) and Lady Poetesses from Hell (science fiction and fantasy poetry).

She is a member of the Science Fiction and Fantasy Writers of America and the National Writers Union. In 1991 the NWU became part of the UAW. Finally, years after leaving Detroit, Ms. Arnason became an auto worker.

She has no idea why she wrote this bio in the third person, but she did.

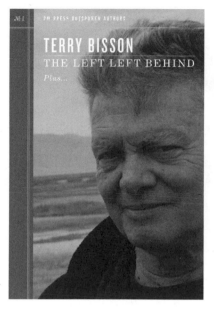

PM PRESS
OUTSPOKEN AUTHORS

The Left Left Behind
Terry Bisson
978-1-60486-086-3
$12

Hugo and Nebula award-winner Terry Bisson is best known for his short stories, which range from the southern sweetness of "Bears Discover Fire" to the alienated aliens of "They're Made out of Meat." He is also a 1960s New Left vet with a history of activism and an intact (if battered) radical ideology.

The *Left Behind* novels (about the so-called "Rapture" in which all the born-agains ascend straight to heaven) are among the bestselling Christian books in the U.S., describing in lurid detail the adventures of those "left behind" to battle the Anti-Christ. Put Bisson and the Born-Agains together, and what do you get? *The Left Left Behind*—a sardonic, merciless, tasteless, take-no-prisoners satire of the entire apocalyptic enterprise that spares no one-predatory preachers, goth lingerie, Pacifica radio, Indian casinos, gangsta rap, and even "art cars" at Burning Man.

Plus: "Special Relativity," a one-act drama that answers the question: When Albert Einstein, Paul Robeson, J. Edgar Hoover are raised from the dead at an anti-Bush rally, which one wears the dress? As with all Outspoken Author books, there is a deep interview and autobiography: at length, in-depth, no-holds-barred, and all-bets-off: an extended tour though the mind and work, the history and politics of our Outspoken Author. Surprises are promised.

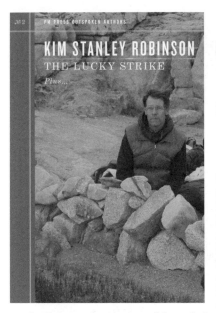

PM PRESS
OUTSPOKEN AUTHORS

The Lucky Strike
Kim Stanley Robinson
978-1-60486-085-6
$12

Combining dazzling speculation with a profoundly humanist vision, Kim Stanley Robinson is known as not only the most literary but also the most progressive (read "radical") of today's top-rank SF authors. His bestselling Mars Trilogy tells the epic story of the future colonization of the red planet, and the revolution that inevitably follows. His latest novel, *Galileo's Dream*, is a stunning combination of historical drama and far-flung space opera, in which the ten dimensions of the universe itself are rewoven to ensnare history's most notorious torturers.

The Lucky Strike, the classic and controversial story Robinson has chosen for PM's new Outspoken Authors series, begins on a lonely Pacific island, where a crew of untested men are about to take off in an untried aircraft with a deadly payload that will change our world forever. Until something goes wonderfully wrong.

Plus: *A Sensitive Dependence on Initial Conditions*, in which Robinson dramatically deconstructs "alternate history" to explore what might have been if things had gone differently over Hiroshima that day.

As with all Outspoken Author books, there is a deep interview and autobiography: at length, in-depth, no-holds-barred and all-bets-off: an extended tour though the mind and work, the history and politics of our Outspoken Author. Surprises are promised.

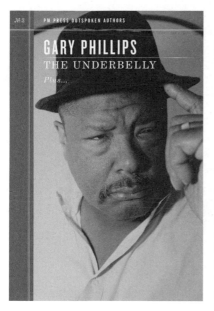

PM PRESS
OUTSPOKEN AUTHORS

The Underbelly
Gary Phillips
978-1-60486-206-5
$12

The explosion of wealth and development in downtown L.A. is a thing of wonder. But regardless of how big and shiny our buildings get, we should not forget the ones this wealth and development has overlooked and pushed out. This is the context for Phillips' novella *The Underbelly*, as a semi-homeless Vietnam vet named Magrady searches for a wheelchair-bound friend gone missing from Skid Row - a friend who might be working a dangerous scheme against major players. Magrady's journey is a solo sortie in which the flashback-prone protagonist must deal with the impact of gentrification; take-no-prisoners community organizers; an unflinching cop from his past in Vietnam; an elderly sexpot out for his bones; a lusted-after magical skull; chronic-lovin' knuckleheads; and the perils of chili cheese fries at midnight. Combining action, humor and a street level gritty POV, *Underbelly* is illustrated with photos and drawings.

Plus: a rollicking interview wherein Phillips riffs on Ghetto Lit, politics, noir and the proletariat, the good negroes and bad knee-grows of pop culture, Redd Foxx, and Lord Buckley, and wrestles with the future of books in the age of want.

"Moorcock crosses genres, bends boundaries, and breaks rules as only a master storyteller can."
—LIBRARY JOURNAL

PM PRESS
OUTSPOKEN AUTHORS

Modem Times 2.0
Michael Moorcock
978-1-60486-308-6
$12

As the editor of London's revolutionary New Worlds magazine in the swinging sixties, Michael Moorcock has been credited with virtually inventing modern Science Fiction: publishing such figures as Norman Spinrad, Samuel R. Delany, Brian Aldiss and J.G. Ballard.

Moorcock's own literary accomplishments include his classic *Mother London*, a romp through urban history conducted by psychic outsiders; his comic Pyat quartet, in which a Jewish antisemite examines the roots of the Nazi Holocaust; *Behold The Man*, the tale of a time tourist who fills in for Christ on the cross; and of course the eternal hero Elric, swordswinger, hellbringer, and bestseller.

And now Moorcock's most audacious creation, Jerry Cornelius--assassin, rock star, chronospy and maybe-Messiah—is back in *Modem Times 2.0*, a time twisting odyssey that connects 60s London with post-Obama America, with stops in Palm Springs and Guantanamo. *Modem Times 2.0* is Moorcock at his most outrageously readable—a masterful mix of erudition and subversion.

Plus: a non-fiction romp in the spirit of Swift and Orwell, Fields of Folly; and an Outspoken Interview with literature's authentic Lord of Misrule.

FRIENDS OF

In the two years since its founding—and on a mere shoestring—PM Press has risen to the formidable challenge of publishing and distributing knowledge and entertainment for the struggles ahead. With over 40 releases in 2009, we have published an impressive and stimulating array of literature, art, music, politics, and culture. Using every available medium, we've succeeded in connecting those hungry for ideas and information to those putting them into practice.

Friends of PM allows you to directly help impact, amplify, and revitalize the discourse and actions of radical writers, filmmakers, and artists. It provides us with a stable foundation from which we can build upon our early successes and provides a much-needed subsidy for the materials that can't necessarily pay their own way. You can help make that happen—and receive every new title automatically delivered to your door once a month—by joining as a Friend of PM Press. Here are your options:

> • $25 a month: Get all books and pamphlets plus 50% discount on all webstore purchases.
> • $25 a month: Get all CDs and DVDs plus 50% discount on all webstore purchases.
> • $40 a month: Get all PM Press releases plus 50% discount on all webstore purchases
> • $100 a month: Superstar—Everything plus PM merchandise, free downloads, and 50% discount on all webstore purchases.

For those who can't afford $25 or more a month, we're introducing Sustainer Rates at $15, $10 and $5. Sustainers get a free PM Press t-shirt and a 50% discount on all purchases from our website.

Just go to **WWW.PMPRESS.ORG** to sign up. Your card will be billed once a month, until you tell us to stop. Or until our efforts succeed in bringing the revolution around. Or the financial meltdown of Capital makes plastic redundant. Whichever comes first.

PM PRESS was founded at the end of 2007 by a small collection of folks with decades of publishing, media, and organizing experience. PM cofounder Ramsey Kanaan started AK Press as a young teenager in Scotland almost 30 years ago and, together with his fellow PM Press coconspirators, has published and distributed hundreds of books, pamphlets, CDs, and DVDs. Members of PM have founded enduring book fairs, spearheaded victorious tenant organizing campaigns, and worked closely with bookstores, academic conferences, and even rock bands to deliver political and challenging ideas to all walks of life. We're old enough to know what we're doing and young enough to know what's at stake.

We seek to create radical and stimulating fiction and nonfiction books, pamphlets, t-shirts, visual and audio materials to entertain, educate and inspire you. We aim to distribute these through every available channel with every available technology - whether that means you are seeing anarchist classics at our bookfair stalls; reading our latest vegan cookbook at the café; downloading geeky fiction e-books; or digging new music and timely videos from our website.

PM PRESS is always on the lookout for talented and skilled volunteers, artists, activists and writers to work with. If you have a great idea for a project or can contribute in some way, please get in touch.

PM PRESS
PO Box 23912
Oakland CA 94623
510-658-3906
www.pmpress.org